Three-times Golden Heart® Award
finalist **Tina Beckett** learned to
pack her suitcases almost before she
learned to read. Born to a military
family, she has lived in the United
States, Puerto Rico, Portugal and
Brazil. In addition to travelling,
Tina loves to cuddle with her pug,
Alex, spend time with her family,
and hit the trails on her horse. Learn
more about Tina from her website,
or 'friend' her on Facebook.

Also by Tina Beckett

Rafael's One Night Bombshell
The Doctors' Baby Miracle
Tempted by Dr Patera
The Billionaire's Christmas Wish
One Night to Change Their Lives
The Surgeon's Surprise Baby
A Family to Heal His Heart
A Christmas Kiss with Her Ex-Army Doc
Miracle Baby for the Midwife
One Hot Night with Dr Cardoza

Discover more at millsandboon.co.uk.

RISKING IT ALL FOR THE CHILDREN'S DOC

TINA BECKETT

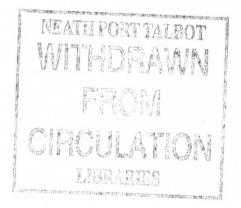

MILLS & BOON

First published in Great Britain 2020
by Mills & Boon, an imprint of HarperCollins*Publishers*
1 London Bridge Street, London, SE1 9GF

Large Print edition 2021

© 2020 Tina Beckett

ISBN: 978-0-263-28752-3

MIX
Paper from
responsible sources
FSC **FSC™ C007454**

This book is produced from independently certified FSC™ paper to ensure responsible forest management. For more information visit www.harpercollins.co.uk/green.

Printed and bound in Great Britain
by CPI Group (UK) Ltd, Croydon, CR0 4YY

To my supportive husband and family!
Thanks for sticking with me!

PROLOGUE

FIVE-YEAR-OLD ELEAZAR ROHAL'S mom kneeled in front of him and took hold of his shoulders. He couldn't remember the words she said, but he could remember the exact moment his universe changed forever. His gaze took in the serious men who stood on either side of her—men whose expressions made him fearful—and the way his mom's mouth trembled when she said she had to go away for a while.

He glanced to the side where his "Aunt Maddie" stood in the doorway and surveyed the scene, tears streaming down her face. When his mom finally stood, she nodded at Maddie, who came over and took his hand. Ellis shook it off, trying to move toward his mom instead. But she took a step back, staying just out of reach.

He stopped. "Mommy?"

"Be good, Ellis. Remember Mommy loves you. Now and forever."

Except she didn't, or she would have stayed with him.

Five years went by. Then Ten. And although Maddie was kind and loving, Ellis had never quite been able to erase the pain generated by his mother's abrupt departure or the fear that Maddie, too, might be taken away by people he didn't know. His questions about whether his mom was in jail or had been kidnapped had been evaded, and Maddie had simply repeated the words she'd said countless times before: Mommy had had to go away, but she would never stop loving him.

He never really believed it. And Ellis could never quite muster up feelings of love for anyone else. *Attachment disorder.* He'd heard the words whispered from behind closed doors. And although the label had eventually fallen away as he threw himself into school—excelling at subjects that involved science and objective reasoning—he never quite forgot what it meant: he was incapable of attaching to others in an emotional way.

But it was okay. He'd found other ways to cope. He'd done his best to banish the possibility of softer emotions—and had been quite successful, if his failed juvenile romances were any indication.

And now on the cusp of graduating from high school and moving into adulthood, he had some decisions to make.

All he knew was that he *would* figure out where he belonged in this world and take his place in it.

No matter how many years it took, or how many sacrifices he had to make to do it.

CHAPTER ONE

LYRIC WESTPHAL WAS LATE. Her phone's alarm hadn't gone off this morning and the shift from Pacific time to Eastern had totally screwed up her body's natural rhythm. And Atlanta had a completely different feel from Las Vegas. But this opportunity had seemed like a gift from heaven for both her and Alia, giving them the chance for a new start. Far from the memory of her sister's death and the circumstances behind it.

If only she could get to her appointment.

God, if she ruined her chances here because of her own lack of foresight, she would be crushed. She glanced at the seat next to her, where her notebook of ideas sat. Maybe it was too soon, but the hospital deserved to know what they were in for.

She swung into the parking lot of the sprawling hospital, found a spot and jumped from her car, clutching her notebook and heading for the entrance at a sprint. Thank God she'd worn low boots.

As soon as she got confirmation that she had the job and found a place to stay, her parents would fly with Alia, reuniting her with her niece. She never dreamed that at thirty-three years of age she would start a family under these circumstances, but she was already fiercely protective of her young charge. And as her dad's health was not the greatest at the moment, they'd made the joint decision that Alia would live with her. Far from Vegas, where she'd grown up. Far from where Lyric's sister had died.

She shoved through the front door, annoyed when a man stepped almost directly into her path, forcing her to swerve so quickly she dropped her notebook. She started to give him a sideways glance, before shelving it when she noted his tight jaw and raised brow.

Not his fault, Ly.

He bent down to pick up the book, glancing at the open pages as he handed it back to her.

"Thanks," she muttered, turning away to face the information desk in front of her and addressing the attendant. "I'm looking for Dr. Lawson's office—I have an appointment."

The man who'd started to walk away retraced his steps, head swiveling toward her. "Dr. Westphal?"

She blinked. How did he know her name? She didn't know him. She didn't know anyone here. And with those boyish good looks and reddish hair, she would have remembered him. "Yes. I'm Dr. Westphal."

The man glanced at the woman behind the desk. "I'll take her up."

She swallowed. He must work here. Or maybe he was even the hospital administrator. "Are you Dr. Lawson?"

"No. Lucky for you. I was just in his office, though. Waiting on you."

She closed her eyes. "I'm sorry. I know I'm late. It's just… It's been one of those mornings. I would have called, but I was driving and…" She sucked down a deep breath. "I'm Lyric Westphal. And you are…?"

"Ellis Rohal. If you decide to take the position, we'll be working together. I'm head of Pediatrics." He nodded at the notebook she clutched. "I take it that isn't an addition to your résumé, unless drug rehabilitation is an interest of yours?"

Oh, perfect. Not quite the way she would have liked this introduction to take place. He must have read some of what she'd written in her notebook. "It is, actually. I'd hoped to talk to Dr. Lawson about it."

His brows came together. "He's a busy man."

"I'm sure he is. I can assure you that I'm never—well, almost never—late."

"Good to know."

Although one corner of his mouth lifted, there was something brusque about his attitude, almost as if he'd already made a judgment about her without even getting to know her. Hopefully he didn't think *she* had a drug problem.

Maybe she needed to restart this meeting. When he stopped at the elevator and pushed the up button, Lyric held out her hand. "Let's try this again, shall we? Dr. Rohal, I look forward to working with you. *If* I'm offered the position."

There was a tiny hesitation before he took her hand. And when he did, she was sorry she'd gone that route. His grip was warm and firm, the slightest hint of callusing scraping against the sensitive skin of her palm, making her shiver. No way he'd gotten those from handling surgical instruments. He held her gaze, eyes seeming to search her features, before he released her hand in a hurry, for which she was glad. Because her heart was suddenly thumping out some funky rhythms.

Then they were in the elevator heading to the fourth floor with several other people. He didn't speak to her, which made her nerves ratchet even higher than they'd been when she entered those front doors.

She hoped Dr. Lawson wasn't as annoyed as Ellis Rohal seemed to be. Or maybe the good doctor was simply against her being here, although she had no idea why that would be the case. Pediatric endocrinologists weren't a dime a dozen, especially the ones who worked more on the behavioral side of the spectrum, although she dealt with plenty of other issues, as well, including abnormal growth issues and pancreatic insufficiency.

Once off the elevator, they turned a corner, and Ellis's long, easy strides made her feel like she was having to run to keep up. By now her knuckles were clenched around the notebook, and she suddenly regretted bringing it along. Maybe it really was too presumptuous of her to share her ideas before she'd even started working at the hospital. Ellis's attitude made her feel she was being accompanied to the principal's office after doing something naughty. And Lyric had always been kind of a Goody Two-shoes, to the amusement of her childhood friends.

Not so her sister, who'd always been wild and free. Only now did she realize that Tessa had been fighting her own demons.

Dr. Rohal reached a door, gave a quick knock and then entered.

The man inside leaned back in his chair, eyes crinkling in a smile that made her heave a sigh of relief. "Ah, so you found her."

This man sounded glad. The opposite of Dr. Rohal.

"I think maybe she found me." The man said it completely deadpan, as if she hadn't nearly careened into him.

"I'm very sorry for being late."

"Nonsense. I suspected you'd gotten lost. After ten years of being here, I've still been known to take a wrong turn or two. It's a big place."

She smiled, very grateful he'd given her an out. "Yes, it is."

With graying hair and wire-rimmed glasses, Dr. Lawson might have been what most people pictured when they thought of hospital administrators. But there was a softness to his eyes that surprised her. As did his dismissal of her tardiness.

Unlike Dr. Rohal.

She'd thought the head of Pediatrics had left Dr. Lawson's office because he was sure she was a no-show, but he'd actually been sent to find her. That had probably annoyed him even more. He was evidently a man who didn't like his time wasted.

Well, while she'd gotten off on the wrong foot with him, she hoped he'd keep an open mind, especially since they'd be working together if she got the job. A prospect that made her a little queasy at the moment. Had this move been a mistake?

No. She'd promised herself that Alia would not go down the same path as Tessa had.

"Have a seat, and you can tell us a little about what brought you to Atlanta."

She dropped into one of the comfy leather chairs across from the desk, noting that Dr. Rohal remained standing, choosing to lean a shoulder against the wall next to him instead. From her seated position he seemed much taller than he had a few moments earlier, his lanky frame stretching toward the ceiling and calling her attention to those narrowed hips and long legs. Stuff she had no business noticing!

She shifted in her chair, suddenly aware of her own curves, which she'd always tried to play down. As a teenager, she'd wanted to be stick-thin, but her build would never allow for that, even though she tried to jog three miles a day whenever she had the chance.

Here's where things got tricky. She didn't exactly want to admit that she was only here because of an unspoken promise she'd made to raise Alia in a place that was far from where her sister had made so many missteps, one of which had resulted in her death, despite the last trip to rehab. The one Lyric had insisted on. Like other stints in different facilities, it had fallen short. As had Lyric's attempts to help her sister. That's where her notebook came in.

"Well, I actually graduated in Las Vegas, as you can see from my résumé, but I really wanted to come to a larger teaching hospital, where there were more opportunities to serve the community at large. I read about the position here at New Mercy and decided to apply."

"Our vigorous curriculum attracts some of the most promising students in the country. Are you interested in teaching, Dr. Westphal?"

She hesitated. "Please call me Lyric. And, yes, I'm open to teaching at some point, if the opportunity arises. Along with some other ideas." The notebook in her hand felt heavy all of a sudden.

"See, Ellis? Some doctors are willing to take on a few medical students."

"I've taken on my share." The other doctor's expression did not change. At all. No flash of humor. No show of irritation. Unlike when she'd bumped into him downstairs.

Dr. Lawson made a sound that made her smile, although she quickly erased it when the pediatrician aimed a look at her. And right on cue, she saw something sprint across his face. Although whatever it was disappeared as quickly as it had appeared.

"I did use the word *willing*," the administrator said.

Lyric would take on two hundred students if it meant she got this position and could reach her goals. The separation would be hard on her parents, but they understood her reasons and fully supported her. It would also give her dad some time to rest.

Her eyes strayed to the handsome doctor she would be working with if she was hired. She hoped he wouldn't be a problem.

As her glance lingered for a second longer than necessary on his broad shoulders and the craggy lines of his face, she swallowed. Maybe it wasn't him that would have the problem.

No. She'd just gotten out of a dead-end relationship and had no intention of starting something else. With anyone. Her five-year romance—if you could call it that—with Jim Riley had been one of the biggest mistakes of her life. And Alia had to be first and foremost in her life right now. The four-year-old had already been through enough. She needed stability. And love.

If Dr. Lawson was hoping Ellis would respond, he was disappointed. He stood right where he was, not looking in the least concerned.

These two men were good friends. She sensed it, despite Ellis's seeming nonchalance. That also made her uneasy. Dr. Rohal could make things difficult for her, in more ways than one.

"So, Dr.... I mean Lyric. I'd like to think I'm a pretty good judge of character. And your résumé and references are impeccable. I'd like to offer you the position. How much notice do you need to give your current hospital?"

Despite a quick thrill of elation, she tensed. "I've already resigned my position there." She'd had reasons she needed to make that cut swift and final. One of which was Jim. Besides, leaving had spurred her to work hard to find another position. It had also removed the possibility of being known as the doctor whose sister had OD'd on opioids.

"So you can start immediately?"

"Yes. I'll need a day off in about a week when my parents fly down, and I need to find a place to stay and a..." She shook her head, almost blurting out that she'd need to find a day care for Alia. It wasn't that she was hiding the fact that she was raising her niece, but she also didn't want to jinx her chances. Not when she was so close to fulfilling her goal.

"Great. Any questions? Anything else you'd like me to know?"

She swallowed, throwing a quick glance at Ellis before turning her attention back to the administrator. "I've toyed with some ideas for a community drug-abuse-prevention initiative, if you'd care to look at it."

"In that notebook you're carrying?" At her nod, he added, "Indeed I would. Why don't you leave it with me, and I'll glance at it after my scheduled meetings."

"Jack, don't you think we should be careful about just—"

Dr. Lawson cut off Ellis. "We will. But we've got that big grant earmarked for the children's unit. I'd say drug-use prevention could merit at least some of those funds."

Uh-oh. An inner voice told her the pediatrician already had his own plans for the grant money they'd received. She did not want to go head-to-head with him. At least not right away. "Please look it over and make sure it fits in with the hospital's plans for the community. The last thing I want is to seem like I'm coming in here with an agenda."

Ellis's head swiveled toward her.

Okay, so maybe she did have an agenda. But it was important to her.

"I like to know where my hospital staff's interests lie." Dr. Lawson reached a hand toward her, and she put the notebook in it, sending up a quick prayer that her arguments were persuasive and well laid out. Sometimes she let her emotions get ahead of her…at least, according to Jim.

Dr. Lawson's voice broke through her thoughts. "Do you have everything you need?

The hospital has some overnight apartments, if you need to stay in one for a while."

"Thank you. I'm having my furniture shipped to me as soon as I officially have the position. And I do have a place to stay temporarily." She didn't mention that it was a hotel room.

"Like I said, consider the position yours. Let us know if you need help moving in."

Us? Her eyes tracked back to the pediatrician. She seriously doubted he would be willing to help. Besides, she didn't have much more than a set of bedroom furniture, a sofa and a dining-room table, along with a twin bed she'd purchased for Alia. Her mom was going to stay with her for a week or two to help her get settled and to stand in the gap while she looked for a preschool.

"Thanks again. I'm very happy to be here."

"Great. Ellis, can you show Lyric around and take her by Human Resources to finish the process? She'll need a lanyard as well as a sticker for her vehicle."

Lyric glanced again at the head of Pediatrics and found him with a frown. He hadn't known he was going to be playing babysitter and wasn't happy about it. "If you have other things to do, I'm sure someone in HR can give me a map."

"No, it's fine. We need to sit down, anyway, and have a talk about…expectations."

The slight emphasis on that word made a shiver go through her.

"Ellis, you go easy on her. She hasn't even started yet."

He gave the administrator a tight smile. "Don't worry. I plan to treat Dr. Westphal with the same kid gloves as the rest of the staff."

Lawson gave a quick snort of laughter. "That's what I'm afraid of." He turned his attention to Lyric. "Don't worry. His bark is much worse than his bite."

She doubted that. She bet his bite was every bit as bad. Maybe even worse. So what she needed to do was stay out of reach of those pearly whites and concentrate on doing her job until she could prove herself to him. She tossed her head and gave the pediatrician a look. "I'm sure we'll get along just fine."

And she intended to do that. No matter how maddeningly attractive the man was. Or the fact that being "bitten" by him had just taken on a whole new—and entirely dangerous—meaning.

Ellis sucked down a deep breath and tried to hold onto his temper. Temper mostly directed at himself. Ever since he'd run in to the new doctor in the lobby and she'd fastened those darkly lashed eyes on him, he'd been on edge, his attention drawn to her again and again. Even now there was a steely cord that pulled at something in his gut, making him notice little things about her, like the way her nose turned up at the tip and the dot of a beauty mark that sat just beside her left eye.

Not good. He was rarely drawn to anyone, especially not the people he worked with. That character trait—some would say character *flaw*—was so deeply ingrained that it had become comfortable. A safety zone that people didn't venture beyond. Or if they did happen to wander past that boundary, it didn't take long for them to retreat as quickly as they'd come.

The fact that Lawson might look at the ideas in her notebook and decide those were a better use of the funds than the equipment he'd requisitioned…well, that didn't help. The grant money wasn't endless. He'd always been a fan of requesting tangible items that could be used time and time again, rather than programs whose efficacy couldn't be measured or that were a one-time push that would be over in a flash.

Was there a drug problem in Atlanta? Yes, just like every major city across the United States. Did initiatives help? Possibly, but Ellis had always had difficulty with things that were subjective in nature. Another "perk" of his childhood.

"I need to run by my office to get something, and we can have that quick chat while we're there."

She seemed to stiffen beside him. "Listen,

I brought those ideas as just that. Ideas. I'm not trying to take over. I had no way of knowing that the pediatric department had just received a grant."

He believed her. He'd wondered if Jack had mentioned the money during their phone interview. But her gaze was steady. "I was just surprised you brought a proposal with you. Did you spearhead an effort in Las Vegas, as well?"

"No." She paused, her hair sliding forward to hide that freckle beside her eye. "But I wish I'd done more to address the drug problems when I lived there."

Her voice was so soft he almost missed the words.

"May I ask why?"

She shrugged. "Because we can't just rely on rehab programs. People sometimes go through that process multiple times and then fall right back into the same old habits—slide into the same damaged friendships. Rehab programs are a great tool, but they can't be the only one we use. I believe we need to break the cycle of addicts returning to old patterns. We need to help them form new connections. New friendships. Strong ones. Far from the drug culture. Help them find new jobs. Form new patterns of behavior through training, behavioral modification, medication. Whatever it takes."

He'd done the behavioral-modification route as a child. They'd even tried to teach him how to attach to people. But although Maddie had tried, he could see now that she'd been grieving, too, and had been focused on suddenly being thrust into the role of a single mom.

His instinct was to brush past Lyric's words, but she spoke with a conviction that made him stop and take a closer look at her.

"Once Jack is done with your notebook, I'd like to take a look at it, as well. I can't promise to change my mind, and I'll be honest and say that I already have plans for that money."

"I thought maybe you did. It doesn't have to be right away. I just wanted to let people know that this is something I'm passionate about."

His various counselors had been, too. But in the end, old patterns seemed to be too ingrained, the fabric of his life already woven. And now he didn't even try to change that—didn't want to.

He started walking again. "I can tell you are." Ellis thought there might be more to it than what she'd said, but he wasn't going to pry. Not yet. And since she leaned toward behavioral endocrinology, it made sense that she might look at addictive behavior in a way that others might not. His own childhood experiences with behavioral modification were tied to unhappy memories.

Five minutes later, they were in his office, which was a bit more plush than he would have chosen if he'd had any say in the decor. But Jack had reiterated what the higher-ups had already said. They wanted the hospital as a whole to have a welcoming feel. That included any space where one might encounter patients or their families, and since he did meet with people in his office, he really hadn't been able to argue, even if he would have preferred a metal desk and simple folding chairs.

Instead there was a warm brown leather love seat with red throw pillows. He saw her glance trail around the room and wondered how those brown eyes were processing it. Did she see the decor as a waste of funds, like he did?

Finally she blinked and looked back at him. "Very nice."

"Have a seat. How different is New Mercy from your hospital in Las Vegas?"

"Pretty different. Las Vegas is a show world, so I think the city as a whole has a glitzy image to uphold. Including the hospital I worked at."

So her old hospital had been even more ostentatious than New Mercy? "And here I was wondering if you'd be uncomfortable with the money spent on decorating."

She shrugged. "It's part of today's medicine, I think. I'd be just as happy in a supply closet, though."

That surprised him. "So would I."

She smiled. "Wow. It looks like we agree on something. Finally."

Yes, it did, and he wasn't sure how he felt about that. Having an adversarial relationship with her seemed the less complicated path right now. Maybe he should try to hold on to that for as long as possible.

He rounded his desk and dropped into the high-backed office chair. "So it would seem."

They spent the next twenty minutes discussing the normal workings of the hospital and some of the research she'd done on addictive personality disorder. He was surprised that the dopamine used to treat some of the symptoms of Parkinson's were now suspected of causing gambling addictions in some of those same patients.

"I think I knew on some level that there could be a hormonal link in addiction, but I've not studied it enough to form an opinion one way or the other," he said.

He'd often wondered if attachment disorders were a result of more than just childhood trauma. Maybe some people were just wired that way. Like him.

"Behavioral endocrinology is pretty interesting. But it's impossible to say which came first. Drug use can also cause physical changes in the brain, which perpetuate addiction. So after the issue has been dealt with through rehab, a new form of addiction might pop up, like gambling or even eating disorders."

That made sense.

"Someday we'll have to have an in-depth discussion on that." And that had nothing to do with the way her eyes sparkled when she talked, or the way she leaned toward him when trying to make a point. It was almost worth trying to play devil's advocate just to keep the conversation going, except he didn't want to like anything about her. He hadn't been in favor of hiring her in the first place, felt like the department ran pretty smoothly without adding another cog in the machine.

And he wasn't really interested in changing his opinion just yet.

Time to shift to a different subject. "You mentioned needing to find a place to stay. Have you met with a Realtor yet? Depending on what part of the city you want to live in, one-bedroom apartments are a little harder to find. I could give you the name of the person I used."

"That would be great. But I need a two-bedroom place. Not one."

She sounded like that was nonnegotiable. Was she planning on getting a roommate? Or maybe she had a child. He hadn't even thought of that. Or maybe she just needed an extra room. Whatever her reasons, it was none of his business.

He scrolled through his list of contacts until he reached the right entry. "Do you want to put the number in your phone?"

"Oh, yes, of course." She grabbed her purse and retrieved the phone from a front pocket. "Okay, I'm ready."

He read off the number. "His name is Dave

Butler and he's with Great Properties Real Estate. He's a friend of mine."

"Thank you. I really appreciate it. Any tips about which areas I should look in?"

"It depends on how long you want your commute to be. As you saw this morning, traffic can be heavy."

Her fingers went to a simple stud earring, twisting it one way and then another. "I'm not so much worried about the commute as I am about the…"

"The…?"

"I would like it to be in a good—as in fewer drugs—school system. It won't be as important now as it will be in the next year or so."

The next year?

He knew she was single. That much had come out during his discussion with Jack. But if she was pregnant, shouldn't he know that she might need to take a leave of absence at some point? She hadn't volunteered the information, and he wasn't sure he was even legally allowed to ask about it. If she wanted him—or anyone else to know—she would tell him.

And, in reality, he didn't want to know. The less he knew about Lyric's personal life, the better. He wasn't quite sure why that was the case, but some primal instinct was telling him to keep his distance from this one. Kind of hard to do when he would be working so closely with her. Possibly even warring with her about how that grant money was going to be spent.

But still…

"Is there something I should know?" he asked.

The fingers fiddling with her ear paused for a few seconds—seconds that told him volumes, although she probably didn't realize it. She didn't want to tell him, but was trying to think through her decision.

"Maybe. I didn't mention it, because I don't anticipate it affecting my work in any major way."

She took a deep breath and then the words

came out so fast his brain had time processing them.

"I have a four-year-old who'll need to be enrolled in a good preschool."

CHAPTER TWO

A QUICK SUCCESSION of emotions scrolled across his face, the last of which was shock. "You have a…child?"

She forced her hand away from her ear and back into her lap, then clasping her hands tightly "Yes. And no. She's my niece. She'll be living with me—permanently. My mom will be bringing her as soon as I find a place to live. Which is why I want to locate a preschool that's not too far from my apartment."

This was something she'd be having to explain time and time again. But it was probably important for him to know where she was coming from. She twined her fingers together until they hurt, willing herself not to let him see the chaotic frenzy of emotions that were tumbling through her system. "My sister died of a drug overdose six months ago. I've been helping to care for her child on and off ever since she was born."

He leaned forward, planting his elbows on his desk. "I'm sorry. I had no idea."

The earnest words, coming from a man who'd seemed hard as nails for most of their hour together, caused a dangerous prickling sensation to gather behind her eyes. Damn. She did not want to cry in front of him. She wanted to be just as distant and unreachable as he seemed to be, except she just wasn't good at playing those kinds of games.

And she missed her sister. So very badly. Had missed her even before she died.

"Tessa went through various rehab facilities and nothing seemed to stick. Her experiences were why I changed my focus from simple pediatric endocrinology to behavioral endocrinology. If some of my sister's addiction patterns could have been redirected while she was still in her teens or even younger, maybe her life wouldn't have played out like it had. And I want to make sure Tessa's daughter doesn't feel abandoned. Either by me or by the system."

"Abandoned. I can see how she might feel that way."

Did he? Or was he just giving a conventional response because he didn't know what else to say? But when she looked into his green eyes, there was a dark flash of something she didn't understand. She chalked it up to an unattached man who had no clue about the struggles people like Tessa, or now, Alia, went through.

Except she didn't know if he was unattached. Nor did she care.

"So that's why I'm so interested in looking beyond the hospital and into the community, to see how I can make a difference."

"And if you can't make a difference?"

His words stopped her in her tracks. Was that what he thought? That it was a hopeless cause? She hoped not, because they definitely would not get along if that was the case. What it *would* do, however, was make her second-guess her decision to move to Atlanta and apply at this hospital.

"What do you think the answer is, then?"

"I have no idea, honestly. I treat the patients who cross my path. Period."

She blinked. Did he even realize how cold that sounded?

"So you have no interest in trying to change things? In trying to prevent some of those patients from ever needing to cross your path?"

"It's not that I'm not interested. I would just need to look at studies before diving into something I have no knowledge of."

Some of the tension drained from her. So it wasn't that he refused to get involved. He just didn't know anything about what she was trying to do. "I do have some statistics in my proposal, but you'll find it a bit of a nature-nurture paradox. Sometimes we can only effect change if we experiment with different methods. It's how some of our greatest advances in medicine came about."

"I'll be interested in looking at the numbers." He didn't sound entirely convinced, but then she didn't expect him to be. She would be the first to admit that she had a very personal reason for her interest in drug prevention. Ellis didn't come across as someone who was driven by emotion. Had he never experienced a heartache strong enough to motivate him to change something?

"That's all I'm asking for. I don't know the hospital or the community yet, so it may not even fit in what would work in this area. I plan on researching what's currently being done. Maybe my ideas would be redundant. If so, I'll accept that and be happy that there's work being done."

Lyric had done some research even before her trip to Atlanta. She thought there was room for a new approach, but Atlanta was turning out to be very different from Las Vegas. She had actually shared her ideas with her own hospital before she left, but obviously she would no longer be there to fight for them. And that didn't sit well. But Alia had to be her number-one priority for now.

Maybe in the future, she could go back to

her home city and try to advocate for change. Only time would tell. But for now she was here. In Atlanta. And she would help where she could.

She thought of something. "Can I ask what you earmarked the grant money for?"

"New equipment. Updated record-keeping procedures."

Her head tilted. "Nothing for the patients themselves?"

"I'm sorry? Those would benefit the patients."

Maybe. But she would have expected at least one thing that addressed patient comfort, especially in the pediatric ward.

"Can I make a suggestion?"

"Another one?" But the smile he gave her took the sting out of the words.

She smiled back. "I could always make up another proposal."

"Not necessary." He leaned back in his chair, his gaze catching hers. "Let's hear it."

"Maybe something fun for the kids. Hospitals are already a stressful place. Is there anything we could do to ease their stay?"

"Other than trying to provide accommodations for the families?"

"Yes. Things like therapy animals. A visiting magician. Recognition of birthdays. Updated—as in brighter—decor in the hallways." She'd noticed there weren't very many things that set this wing apart from the other ones. "Maybe even have themes for the different sections of Pediatrics."

"Themes." He picked up a pencil and scribbled something on a pad. "I tend to think more in terms of actual physical benefits."

"I think some of those things would provide actual physical benefits. While also benefiting their emotional well-being."

"So says some of the other staff."

So people had already brought this up to him. If so, as a newbie, she probably wouldn't be the one to change his mind. "I'm not sure what your grant amount was, but surely a few hundred dollars could be used toward enrichment."

"Three million." He said it without a flicker of emotion. Not even the twitch of an eyebrow.

"Your grant is three million dollars?"

"It is."

Her brain swirled with possibilities, but she knew that in the end the decision wasn't up to her. It was up to him and, ultimately, the board of directors as to who would decide where the money should be spent.

As if realizing where her thoughts were going, he laid down his pen. "I can see that I may come to rue the day the hospital hired you."

Shock overtook her before she realized he was joking. It was there in the slightest twitch of those firm lips.

She laughed. "Then I will make it my mission in life to make sure you don't. And I do vow not to suggest a karaoke korner—corner spelled with a *k*—featuring show tunes."

"Surely that isn't actually a thing."

He tilted his head in a way that suggested he was flabbergasted by that notion, and he now looked almost too gorgeous for words. She swallowed, remembering the callused palm that had slid across hers earlier.

"Surely it is. And I'll be the first to admit that the kids love it. Especially the ones in the oncology ward."

"Karaoke korner…okay."

And without knowing why, she laughed again, realizing she might have waded into waters that were a little deeper than she'd expected. Time to trudge her way back toward shore, where the sand was firm and where her feet were far less likely to be pulled out from under her by some rogue wave. Like the one seated across from her, whose sudden smile threatened to do just that: pull her under. Way, way under.

Karaoke korner.

Exactly what kind of hospital had Lyric come from? One very different from New Mercy, that was for sure. Was he that much of a stick-in-the-mud? It looked like she thought he was. So did a lot of other people on his staff, but he really hadn't cared. His bottom line was saving lives.

But she claimed that those other things could help do that, as well. He'd shown her around and left her in the HR department to finish up some routine paperwork. But as he had, he'd been very aware of the plain walls in the corridors. Walls that, every once in a while, were punctuated with some kind of framed art. But even those pictures that were fun had a common theme: education. Frogs displaying healthy eating habits. Lions that suggested patients get out there and lead active lives. Not a karaoke korner in sight.

But maybe there should be. Not with show tunes. But kids songs? And fun games?

Something he'd not experienced a whole lot of during his childhood. Maddie had worked hard to provide for them, but it hadn't left much time for other things. Like vacations. Or birthday parties. Or Valentine's Day cards for his classmates.

Was that why he'd been so opposed to some of his colleagues' suggestions over the past several years? Because it reminded him of things he'd missed out on? And along comes Lyric and does just that.

Hell, what had he just let into his department?

He could almost swear that those second thoughts came from learning that Lyric was taking in her niece. A girl that, if he had to guess, had been abandoned, emotionally and physically, thanks to her mom's drug habit.

Ellis couldn't remember a lot about his own mother, but he could swear she was not a drug user. And his dad? There was nothing. He couldn't remember a time when a man had been around, and Maddie once told him even she didn't know who his father was.

He'd often wondered if his mom had become a spy or something for the government. But surely she would have eventually come back to find him or try to reestablish contact if that was the case. She never had. And Maddie had died when Ellis was in his early twenties, leaving him with questions that would never be answered. What she had left him, however, was a trust fund that had been established by his mom. It hadn't been an astronomical figure, but having sat in the bank for a decade and a half, it had accrued a healthy amount of interest.

Which again ruled out drug use and prison, because he'd looked through the national database of prisons, looking for her name, but nothing had matched.

He sighed, irritated that these old thoughts had come back to haunt him. Could it be that he sensed a hurt in Lyric that rivaled the hurt he'd once felt over his mom's disappearance from his life? But his emotions over the past had gone cold long ago, while hers were still raw and painful. Her niece would be a constant reminder of what had happened to her sister. Probably the way Maddie had been a reminder that his real mother had left him without a single explanation.

A twinge in his chest jarred him, and he rubbed a palm across it. He didn't want to go back and relive any of that. So, time to think about keeping a bit of distance between him and the hospital's newest staff member. Any changes he implemented in his department would be because he felt they were needed, and not to make one Lyric Westphal happy.

Even as he thought it, he took out his phone and called his Realtor friend. The two of them had known each other since high school and had kept in touch over the years. Ellis didn't have a ton of friends, but he counted Dave among the closest. He'd asked Lyric if she minded if he gave Dave her contact information and she'd thanked him, saying she'd appreciate that.

"Hey, Ellis. I hoped I'd hear from you. You never gave me an answer about the game next week."

Damn, he'd forgotten about that. "Sorry, you're right. I've just been swamped. When is it again?"

He got through the preliminaries and agreed to go with his friend to the Braves game next week. He then gave a quick rundown on what Lyric said she was looking for, leaving out anything personal, like her sister's death.

"Ah, new love interest, buddy?"

And just like that, he regretted making the call. "No. You know me. I'm not interested in going that route." It wasn't that he hadn't gone out on dates or slept with his share of women. He had. But he'd never had a serious relationship and had no desire for one at this point in his life. Love and kids just weren't in the cards for him.

"Smart guy." Dave was divorced and had sworn over a few too many beers that he was never going down the aisle again. Although Ellis didn't believe him for a minute.

"So if you could give Lyric a call and steer her in the right direction—"

"Pretty name."

Yes, it was, but he wasn't about to admit that or the fact that he'd noticed a little more about her than he should have. He didn't need his friend getting the wrong idea and saying something to her. "I guess. She seems to be a competent physician. That's all I care about."

He didn't actually know how good of a doctor she was yet, but her résumé was impeccable and Jack would have checked her references. The hospital administrator was genuinely nice, but he was no pushover and didn't put up with poor performances from his staff.

"Stacy and I just broke up, you know. It was for the best, but about this new doc, any chance she's—"

"Dave…" He let a warning note creep into his voice. The last thing he wanted was for his friend to be unprofessional, especially after Ellis was the one who'd recommended the Realtor in the first place.

"Ah. Got it. Don't worry, I won't hit on your girl."

"She is not my girl." His voice tightened further.

Dave laughed. "Calm down, or I'm really going to start wondering."

"Don't make me regret giving her your name." He forced his voice to lighten. He knew it was just Dave's personality to joke, and had no idea why he was overreacting to it now. Maybe because something about Lyric made him bristle.

"I won't. Scout's honor."

With that they said goodbye and Ellis dropped his cell phone back onto the desk, wondering over the crazy day he'd already had. And with the full slate of appointments he had scheduled, it wasn't going to let up anytime soon. Putting Lyric and Dave firmly out of his mind, he concentrated on what he could control.

Medicine. He sighed and pulled the nearest case file toward him. It wasn't like he always had control of those outcomes, either. But sometimes all he could do was try his hardest and hope for the best.

CHAPTER THREE

TWO DAYS AFTER her furniture had been delivered, Lyric studied the radiographed images she'd received. They were of a child's left hand and wrist, with hormone test results slated to arrive sometime this afternoon.

She was pretty sure she knew what the results would show. That Jacob Sellers would need a little help catching up to his classmates. In the bottom one percentile of the norms for children his age, it was a good thing his parents hadn't waited to have him tested. Left untreated, he would fall further and further behind, and once his growth plates closed, there would be no chance of catching up. Unfortunately, treatment would include a daily shot—no fun for anyone—and she'd already called and left a voice mail for

Ellis to update Jacob's family, since he was the one who'd called for a consult on the case.

Her meeting with Ellis's friend, Dave Butler, had resulted in her finding a cute little town house in only a day. She would rent it until she could find a place to actually buy. And the best part was, there was a preschool within walking distance. That would be hard to top. She'd told Dave to keep his ears open, but that she was in no big hurry to put in an offer on something else.

He'd been nice, and when their conversation turned to Ellis, who was a high-school friend of his, it had been hard not to be curious. She'd done her best not to ask any kind of personal questions, but she would love to know if he was always so... She wasn't even sure of the word she'd use to describe him— reserved with a touch of surly, maybe? Or if he was only that way with her. If Lyric had to guess, she would say that she wasn't his first choice as an addition to his department. Dave did say, however, that he doubted Ellis would ever marry.

She wasn't even sure how that subject had come up, but she'd squashed it the best she could. Especially since she didn't want Dave going back to Ellis with tales of how interested she'd been in his personal life. Plus, there was the fact that she'd probably be talking to Dave quite a bit more as he researched properties for her. Better to set the tone now, rather than be sorry later.

Her mom had gotten a great price on flights, and she and Alia were due to arrive this morning. She was going to come to the hospital and pick up keys to Lyric's place and then work on getting Alia settled in her new bedroom. Lyric's mom had bought some jungle-themed posters and bedding, and brought them along with them. It would give them something to do while Lyric was at work, anyway. And it would help her niece feel she'd had some input into what her room looked like.

Lyric's heart cramped. It should be Tessa who was sharing these special moments with Alia. It was so hard to believe she'd never see her sister again. She closed her eyes to blot out that thought, then stretched her back and shut down the screen of her laptop. Someone knocked at her door, and she stiffened for a second, before calling to whoever it was to come in.

Ellis entered her tiny office. "I got your message. So I was right to refer the patient to you?"

Was that supposed to be a rhetorical question? "The radiographs of his hand do seem to support the insufficiency of growth hormones. I'm just waiting on the results of the blood tests."

The problem with measuring growth hormones in the human body was that they were released in pulses, so if blood was drawn at the wrong time, there might be a false negative. So Lyric had administered medication geared to stimulate the release of those hormones. To see if there were still lower than expected levels that, along with the hand and wrist X-rays, would indicate intervention was warranted.

"Good. When I talked to his parents, they seemed in favor of hormone therapy."

"Yes, they mentioned that to me, as well, when I spoke with them on the phone. I think they were glad to know the problem wasn't just in their imagination. And that there might be some treatment options."

Ellis rounded the nearest chair and lowered himself into it, his knees nearly touching the front of her desk. "Good. Let me know what his blood test shows."

"I will." Wow, the man made her already small space seem minuscule. He could just reach across her desk and…

And nothing.

Remember that wave, Lyric. You need to stick close to shore.

"Dave said you found a place?"

She hesitated, hoping that Dave wasn't as free in sharing his observations of her as he had been about Ellis. Not that she'd encouraged him. She hadn't. The Realtor had only gotten in a few brief summaries before she'd done her best to halt the subject. "I did—

thanks for recommending him. He seems very…efficient."

Efficient? Really, Ly?

Ellis studied her face for a moment or two, and right on cue, she felt a surge of heat zip through her cheeks.

"Hmmm…maybe I shouldn't say anything, but Dave divorced a few months ago. And he just broke up with a girlfriend."

More heat scorched through her. Was he hinting that she should go out with his friend? Not happening. He wasn't really her type. She was more into… Her eyes tracked to Ellis. Oh, Lord.

"I don't think that's any of my—"

"Sorry. You're right. It's just that Dave sometimes acts before he thinks."

Unlike Ellis? She could very well believe that the pediatrician did nothing without mulling it over in his brain for a few thousand years.

Like Jim? No. Lyric's ex hadn't been merely cautious about deepening their relationship. He just hadn't been interested.

At all.

He'd been perfectly happy hooking up peri-odically and letting the rest just coast along. The day her sister died, he'd sent her a "con-dolence" text. The pain of that had been the last straw. She'd called him and broken it off, asking him not to come to the funeral. She couldn't carry a relationship on her own, and she'd been done trying.

As for Ellis, she had no idea how he han-dled relationships, nor did she care.

"I think we can all be guilty of impulsiv-ity from time to time." Acting before she thought was probably how her sister had got-ten hooked on drugs. It had made Lyric more careful about following her impulses. Not that she would ever be tempted to do drugs. Far from it. Even the time she'd hurt her back and her doctor had wanted to prescribe pain med-ication had been met with an upheld hand. No bones had been broken, so she'd relied on ibuprofen to help her get through the next couple of weeks.

"Maybe." Ellis's dubious tone made her

more certain that he didn't want to be numbered among the people who bought candy in the checkout lane of his local grocery store. Or asked a woman out after meeting her for the first time. "I wanted to talk to you about something else, though."

Something besides Jacob Sellers? Maybe Dave really had said something that wasn't meant for public consumption. Her finger went to her earlobe, but since she'd forgotten to wear earrings today, she found nothing to twirl. She dropped her hand back to the desk. It was a bad habit, anyway. Good thing she didn't play poker, or she'd be broke in a matter of days.

"O-o-k-a-a-ay." She drew the word out. "What is it?"

"Jack wants a more in-depth proposal on your antidrug initiative. One geared specifically for the greater Atlanta area. And he wants me in on it. We're supposed to take a couple of days and research what's already being done, taking one or two of those days to do a physical search of a couple of corridors known for their drug use."

"He does?" Shock went through her. She remembered the hospital administrator wanting to look through her idea notebook, but had expected nothing would come of it. Especially since Ellis had said he already had plans for the grant money. Did that mean he'd changed his mind? Or was he being forced to do something he didn't agree with? Maybe she should address that. "And you're onboard with this?"

Ellis propped an ankle on his left knee. "Let's just say I'm willing to keep an open mind."

She glanced at him, noting the slight furrow between his eyebrows. She wasn't sure if the frown indicated thoughtfulness or irritation. It did nothing to reduce his "wow" factor, though. If anything, it just made him more mysterious and harder to read. She'd bet this man had women throwing themselves at him from every corner.

And yet Dave had said it was doubtful he would ever marry.

Oh, no. You are not heading back to that subject, Ly. Because you are definitely not in the market for anyone, either.

Especially not with her young niece coming to live with her. She couldn't afford having someone who would pop in and out of her life at their leisure.

Still, her eyes slid down his straight nose and landed on his lips before she jerked her gaze to a philodendron she'd inherited from the office's last occupant. Man, she needed to water that thing. Its leaves were starting to wilt.

She forced herself to recall what he'd just said. Open mind. Okay. That she could deal with. "That's all I ask."

"I'm sure it's not easy to go into these kinds of things with hard fact and not let your emotions get wrapped up, especially since—"

"You're right. My sister was the reason I started thinking about this. She's even the reason that I decided to make the switch to behavioral endocrinology, but everything I've read or studied just reinforces the idea that we need to gear our efforts to a younger segment of the population."

She doubted Ellis let his emotions "get wrapped up" in anything.

"How young?"

"Well, certainly before they reach eighteen." She made a motion in the air. "It's kind of like Jacob Sellers's bones. We need to intervene before those growth plates close, to have the best chance at changing course. Once closed, those bones become set in stone. Literally. The longer a person uses drugs, the harder it is to change those habits. They become hardwired into our grey matter."

His propped foot jiggled a time or two, bringing her thoughts back to him as a person. From his perpetually mussed hair, to his strong thighs and narrow hips, he was put together in a way that defied logic and made it hard not to notice him. Lord, why couldn't he be some weaselly man with a nasal twang and twenty kids?

"Good comparison. And it makes sense. But we have a definitive treatment protocol for patients like Jacob. But drugs…"

"I know." Any warmth his first remark had generated was wiped away by the dubious tone that came after it. He was right. There was no easy answer. "But we have all kinds of conditions that don't have a cut-and-dried treatment. That doesn't mean we don't keep trying. Think about childhood cancers or even muscular dystrophy. We keep looking, keep researching, in hopes that someday we'll stumble on something that *will* work."

One corner of his mouth tilted. "I think you should have gone into apologetics instead of medicine."

Just like it had at other times, the very hint of a smile made her catch her breath and sent her thoughts spinning out of control.

I doubt Ellis will ever marry.

She banished the thought that somehow kept creeping in. It didn't matter to her one way or the other. "I don't like to argue with people, so that wouldn't be a good match for me." Nor would Ellis be a good match for her...if she were even looking for a man, which she wasn't.

"I haven't found that to be true."

Her teeth came down on her lip. He thought she was argumentative?

As if sensing her thoughts, he added, "You're very good at persuasion."

Okay, *persuasive* put a more positive spin on it. "Only if I truly believe in what I'm fighting for."

He leaned forward. "And what are you fighting for, exactly, Lyric?"

Maybe he'd said her name before, but she couldn't ever remember hearing it roll off someone's tongue in those low gritty tones before. It caught her off guard, making all rational thought crash through her brain's guardrail, making it hard to find anything to say that wouldn't sound crazy. Or overly personal.

Like asking him to say her name again.

"I'm fighting for..." The pause was long enough to become awkward, so she said the first thing that came to mind. "I'm fighting for people like my niece, who've lost a family member to drug use and who are in danger of becoming statistics themselves if there's no one there to catch them. Luckily she has other relatives who love and care for her. Who want her to grow up far from that kind of life."

He gave her a look. "She's one of the lucky ones, then. And the reason you moved from Los Vegas to Atlanta?"

"Yes." It was that simple and that complicated. Alia deserved a chance at normalcy, and each day Lyric prayed she was making the right decision. Every city and town had drug issues, so hopefully she wasn't just trading one problem location for another. "I would do anything for her."

Ellis's eyes met hers, and for several long seconds she couldn't force herself to look away.

"I know you would," he said. "Let me know how I can—"

A soft knock sounded at the door, interrupting whatever he'd been about to say. He stood. "Let me know what Jacob's test results say, and we'll talk about when to take that research trip."

"Okay." She stood as he headed for the door and opened it. Something flew past him so fast that Ellis took a step backward, his head turning to follow its trajectory around the desk until the small form attached itself to Lyric's knees.

"Aunt Lyrie, Aunt Lyrie!" Her niece's mispronunciation of her name had always made her smile and today was no exception.

"Alia, you almost knocked Dr. Rohal down." She sent a quick apologetic glance his way just as her mom appeared in the doorway.

"I'm sorry, honey, I didn't realize you had someone here with you." Her mother's gaze went to Ellis.

"It's okay," he said. "We were just finishing up. You must be Lyric's mom."

"I am. Paula Westphal. And that little tornado is Alia. Sorry for her barging in like that."

"No need to apologize. I'm Ellis Rohal, one of Lyric's colleagues."

Colleagues? More like her boss. He definitely had seniority over her and probably had the power to put the kibosh on her project. Hopefully he wouldn't, though.

Lyric knelt down to hug her niece, wrapping her arms around the little girl and dropping a kiss on top of her head. "I'm so glad to see you, sweetheart."

Her glance came up and found Ellis staring at her with some undecipherable expression. He didn't look mad. If anything, he looked taken aback. Probably from being forced to witness their family reunion.

She mouthed, *sorry.*

Ellis shook his head, mouth cocking up in that half smile that seemed to say "it's okay."

The silent exchange between them seemed intimate, somehow. Like trading secrets that they wanted no one else to hear.

Except these weren't secrets, and there'd been no reason for either of them not to say the words aloud. She suddenly wished they had, because ever since he'd come into her office, there'd been this weird awareness that had shimmered in the air. At least on her side. Ellis probably had had none of those thoughts.

"I'll let you go. If you could give me a buzz when those results come in, I'd appreciate it."

"Of course."

With that he was gone, leaving her alone with her mom and niece.

After going over to close the door, she motioned her mom to the chair Ellis had just vacated, while she scooped up Alia and moved back behind her desk. The child bounced on her lap. "How was your flight, Mom?"

"Good." She laughed. "Wow, do all of the doctors in Atlanta look like that?"

"Look like what?" She feigned ignorance and hoped her mom didn't go getting any strange ideas. She'd been the one who'd dried her tears after her disastrous relationship ended, even as she'd been grieving the loss of Tessa. Lyric would have thought she wouldn't be so quick to push her remaining daughter toward another man.

"Well, like the neon lights of a casino that draws folks for miles."

"Mom!" Her words were meant as an admonishment, except her mother was right. Lyric herself had noticed how gorgeous Ellis was. And as hilarious as it was to hear that fact talked about in Vegas terms, it fit. Because just like those casinos that lured would-be gamblers to come and take a shot at the jackpot, he was unpredictable and as hard to read as the dealer at any blackjack table.

"Am I wrong?"

No, she wasn't. "I don't think Dad would be thrilled to hear you talking about another man that way."

They were just words, though. Because her mom and dad were deeply in love and completely committed to each other. And with his current health problems, they'd grown even closer. Which made it that much harder to understand how Tessa had wound up where she had. She'd grown up in a home that was full of warmth and love, not what you'd expect of an addict. But it just went to show how important it was to provide a safety net outside of the family unit.

"Your father never has to worry and he knows it. Besides, your doctor friend is far too young…for me." She gave her daughter a sideways glance that said it all.

"No. Do not even get that look in your eye." Lyric was still in recovery. Not from Jim, but from the whole idea of love and how much of a crapshoot it all was. She wrapped her arms tighter around Alia, who was busy drawing on the calendar blotter that was on top of Lyric's desk. Good thing she used her phone to keep track of her appointments.

"What look, honey?"

"Ha! You know what look. I have this little munchkin to look after right now, and that's all I care about." Besides, Ellis wasn't the marrying type, according to his friend, and Lyric was no longer the friends-with-benefits type, no matter what she'd settled for in the past.

"Munchkins grow up."

She ignored her mom's remark, and said, "Do you two have time for lunch? Or are you too exhausted from the flight? I can give you the key to the town house, if you just want to go get settled in."

"How long do you have for lunch?"

"About an hour. Time enough to grab a bite and head back to the house, if you want to go that route, although I won't be able to stay long."

"Yes, we'd love it, and I'm sure Alia will want you to personally show her where her room will be. I left our luggage with the nice woman at the information booth in the lobby."

Good thing the child was too young to really understand why Mommy wasn't coming home. There'd been some tears the first several days, but since Alia had spent most of her time with her grandparents and Lyric by that time, it had just been a passing shower. Unlike the grief that Lyric and her parents had experienced. All those regrets…

She forced her brain back to her mom's

comment. "Was the woman young and friendly with dark brown hair?"

"She was. And she had the cutest accent."

Probably the same woman who'd been there the day Lyric had arrived at New Mercy and almost crashed into Ellis. Only three days had gone by since that encounter, and she was already starting to feel strangely at home in her new environment.

Except for with Ellis, who disrupted her nerve impulses in ways she didn't understand. Like when he said her name. Or when he smiled and told her she was persuasive.

All she could do was hope it was due to the newness of everything. Since she'd been born and raised in Vegas, this was her first big move away from home. Combine that with the end of a dead-end relationship, and she was happier than she should have been. The last thing she needed to do was let her mom start filling her head with ideas that didn't belong there. She wanted her daughter happy, and Lyric understood that. But now was not the time.

And Ellis had probably not thought of her that way.

And she didn't think of him that way, either. Nor would she. She just needed to keep her eyes on her two life goals: raising Alia and joining the fight to end an epidemic that was destroying thousands of lives a year and leaving devastation in its wake. It wasn't smallpox or polio and there was no vaccine to prevent its spread. So as hunky as the head of her department was, she would fight him tooth and nail, if need be, if he tried to come between her and reaching those goals.

Two days later, Ellis went with Lyric to talk to Jacob Sellers's parents, although he was beginning to regret that suggestion. Watching Lyric's niece run over and hug her tight had made something in his gut shift. The little girl was about the same age as he had been when his mom left forever. Only this child's mother was dead and his was…

He had no idea what she was. But the impact on him had been the same as if she had died. Maybe worse, since she'd left without explanation or any attempt to contact him in the intervening years.

It had to have been awful for Lyric and her mom to have to somehow explain that Mommy wasn't coming home ever again. Except if she'd been a drug addict for as long as Lyric had said, maybe she'd never been a major presence in her daughter's life, anyway. Not like his mom had been in his.

Just outside of the exam room, he paused. "What was your niece's name again?"

Brown eyes met his, a slight flare of shock entering those dark irises. Or was that his imagination? He wasn't even sure why he'd asked the question. He wasn't likely to ever see the child again, so what did it matter? But it was too late to withdraw the words.

"Her name is Alia."

Alia. He mulled that over for a second or two. The syllables had a melodic lilt to them that fit the smiling little whirlwind that had swooped into her aunt's office and hugged her tight. Kind of like Lyric's name fit her. It was unusual and caught at his senses, making him want to say it. Again and again.

He turned his thoughts to something else before he did just that. "Did you find a preschool?"

"Yes. My mom took her this morning and will pick her up at two. I may need to find a sitter to help with that once my mom goes home."

He nodded. "The hospital has a database of services that provide transportation and after-care programs. Or you could care for the bulk of your appointments in the mornings and reserve afternoons for office work."

"Are you saying I could bring her to work?"

What the hell was he doing? These were all things she could figure out on her own. Without his damn interference. "I'm saying you wouldn't be the only one who did that. And there are always other people around who could watch her for a few minutes here or there."

Her head tilted. "I don't know. I kind of want to keep my private life and work life separate, although it's all pretty new right now. Let me see what I can arrange. Although I will look into the database. Thank you."

Time to cut off this topic of conversation before he did something foolish, like offer to help watch the girl. Not that he would. He dealt with enough children on a daily basis without taking on the child of a colleague.

He wanted to help kids. Probably because of his own childhood issues—although he tried not to explore that train of thought more than necessary. But he made sure he kept that help on the medical side of the spectrum. Periodically watching Alia would not fall on that side, and he would be well served to do what Lyric said she was doing: keep his business life and personal life separate. Although Lyric's antidrug initiative had a little of her private life tossed into the mix, didn't it, since she'd lost her sister to drugs? He wasn't about to point that out, however.

"Shall we?" He motioned to the door of the exam room.

Once inside, they greeted Jacob and his

parents. Ellis let Lyric take the lead, since she was the specialist.

"Well, as you know, the tests did show that Jacob may need a little help with his growth hormones. I wanted to explain what that will entail." She motioned them to seats, while she took the exam stool that was in the room. Ellis opted to stand.

He glanced down at where Lyric was leaning forward, her hands moving as she described the treatment protocol, dark hair shining under the harsh glare of the fluorescent lights. Propping a shoulder against the door, he wondered how things were going with Alia. Hopefully the child was settling in, although it had only been two days since she'd arrived in Atlanta.

Raising a child who wasn't your own was a huge undertaking. He probably hadn't appreciated Maddie's sacrifice enough. And with very little in return, honestly. He hadn't been an easy child. He'd been withdrawn and rebuffed her attempts to hug him. And yet she hadn't turned him over to the foster-care system, which now surprised him. Maddie had also never married. He had no idea whether that was because of him or because she'd never met the right person.

Lyric was Alia's blood relative, though, whereas Maddie had only been a friend of the family. But was it any different? The sacrifices were the same either way.

"We'll use Jacob's weight as a guide for the dosage, but it will have to be given daily with no interruptions to be effective."

"Is it a…um, shot?" Jacob's mom looked a little nervous.

"It is, but it's quick and easy. The hormone comes loaded in a kind of pen that, with a click of a button, injects the medication just under the skin. Some caregivers even wait until the child goes to sleep before swabbing the spot with alcohol and administering the injection. It's a tiny needle."

"What if he cries every time he gets it?"

"I can't promise he won't the first time or two. But it's really a lot easier than it sounds. What we'll probably do is set a date for his first shot and have you bring him in, and we'll help you administer it. We can have a few practice runs with a pincushion so you can get the hang of dialing in the dosage on the side of the pen and then pushing the plunger." She smiled at each of the parents and then patted Jacob on the shoulder. "I'm sure he'll do fine."

If she was as good with her niece as she was in reassuring this young family, she was going to raise a kind and responsible young lady. And if Alia's over-the-top reaction at seeing her aunt was any indication, then the child didn't have the same problems as he used to have with attachments.

Used to have? He still did, although he did finally come to love his Aunt Maddie, and was able to show her affection just before she died of a heart attack.

But that didn't mean it came easy now. It didn't. If Alia came running to him, would he stiffen up and freeze? Teach her that love was something that was rebuffed?

Hell. That was part of the reason he wasn't

going to have a family. He just couldn't run the risk.

Lyric set her laptop on the desk in the room. "There's a video I want you to watch about the process that might make things a little easier to understand." She pressed Play and a canned presentation began to display charts and statistics and ended with a demonstration of the pen itself.

When it was over, there were a few seconds of silence, and Ellis said, "So what do you think? Dr. Westphal has done an admirable job of describing the treatment, but like the video said, it's a long-term commitment. It's better not to do it at all than to start and decide you can't follow through."

Lyric agreed. "I want you to be completely comfortable with your decision whichever way you go."

Jacob's dad spoke up. "If we don't go through with treatment, how far behind will Jacob fall?"

"That's hard to predict, but it's doubtful he would ever catch up. He's not producing enough of the hormone on his own, so as the years go by, he'll fall further behind his peers. If he's comfortable with that and you are, as well, then I don't want to talk you into something you'd prefer not to do."

"Jacob has already mentioned wanting to be tall like his daddy. I don't want to let my fear keep me from giving him the best shot at a successful and happy life."

He understood that. Lyric wasn't letting her fear stop her from raising Alia. And Maddie had tried to do the same with him.

Mrs. Sellers looked at her husband. "I want to do this."

"Yes. So do I. We'll both learn how to give the injections and take turns if need be."

Lyric took one of Jacob's hands. "Will you help Mommy and Daddy with this?"

The boy gave a solemn nod.

"Well, it looks like it's unanimous. I'll look at my calendar and give you a call early this next week for a couple of practice sessions. You can either bring Jacob with you, or practice without him the first few times."

Mrs. Sellers glanced at her husband. "Can you get off work to come while Jacob is in school?"

"I'll make it happen. If you can give me about a week's lead time."

"That won't be a problem," Lyric said. "I'll get in touch with the drug company and check with your insurance to see what they say."

"We'll do this with or without insurance."

Ellis spoke up. "If there's a problem, the hospital has a few funding programs we can explore."

"Thank you so much." Mrs. Sellers clasped her husband's hand.

A few minutes later, they said their goodbyes, and Ellis saw them out the door.

Lyric glanced at her watch. "I think they made the right decision."

"I think *they* think they made the right decision."

"You disagree?" Her head tilted to look up at him.

"No, but if it had gone the other way, would you have been just as supportive?"

She hesitated. "I'll admit, I truly feel it's in that child's best interest to undergo treatment. But they have to buy in, as well, or it won't work."

Maybe it was just the way he was built, but Ellis had always maintained a certain distance from his patients. He rarely got emotionally charged about diagnoses or treatments, always thinking of it as being professional and objective, something they were actually taught in medical school. Lyric was obviously strongly in favor of treatment in this case, but he was pretty sure she wouldn't have overridden the parents' wishes.

And in the end, he agreed with her. He thought it was in Jacob's best interest, too.

She was still looking up at him, and today there was no earring to twirl. He found he missed that. In fact, once or twice he'd had an urge to say or do something that would make her do just that: make those elegant fingers reach for her earlobe.

Hell, he needed to get out of this room before he was tempted to do something besides meet her gaze for gaze. "I do think they'll stick to the treatment protocol. They're dedicated and want to do what they think is right."

"I do as well." She stared at him for another minute before glancing away.

He sucked down a breath. "Okay, I have another patient in a few minutes, so let me know when you schedule their first trial run. I'd like to be here."

Why? There was really no reason to. Was it because of Jacob? Or because of Lyric? Something told him he might not want to go searching for an answer to that question.

"I will."

With a raised hand, he turned and walked out of the room. As he did, he could almost swear he felt her bemused gaze follow him. If so, she wasn't the only one who was bemused. And he needed to shake off whatever was going on with him. And soon. Before he said or did something he couldn't take back.

CHAPTER FOUR

"I WISH YOU didn't have to leave so soon."

Her mom gave her a quick hug. "Me, too, but your dad has been holding down the fort for the last week and he has a doctor's appointment coming up. We both plan to visit during the summer. He's already put in for some vacation time. If that's okay."

"Of course it's okay." Her mom had insisted on sleeping on the sofa bed, despite Lyric's repeated offers to take her bed. Maybe she should tell Dave to look for a three-bedroom place instead so she could have an actual guest room. Or she could set up a cot for herself in Alia's room so her parents could have her room.

She'd already offered to take her mom to the airport, but she wouldn't hear of it, saying a taxi would keep Lyric from getting to her meeting late and that if Alia's preschool called she wouldn't be so far away.

Lyric was due to meet Ellis at a local coffee shop to plan their research trip. When she'd suggested meeting in one of their offices, he'd said it might be better to meet where things at the hospital wouldn't interfere and there'd be no interruptions. And he was right. Whenever she stayed home on her days off, things at home tended to pull at her and she ended up working all day instead of taking some much needed time off.

But she had to admit, she was a little nervous. This would be the first time she'd spent much time with him since that day in her office when Alia had arrived. And she'd had a weird reaction to him that day, which she'd chalked up to her imagination. At least she hoped that's all it was, because Jacob Sellers's parents were due to come in a couple of days from now for their trial run of administering the growth hormone. And for some reason, Ellis wanted to be there.

Didn't he trust her?

A horn honked out in front of the town house. "I think that's the taxi." Her mom gave her a tight squeeze. "Tell Alia we'll be back to see her soon."

Her mom had already told the child that. Several times, but there'd still been some tears from her niece on the way to preschool. If it weren't for Lyric's dad's job, she had a feeling her mom would already have her bags packed to move to Atlanta. And maybe that would even help with her dad's heart problems.

As it was, if things went well with things at the hospital, her dad might just put in for a transfer. Or take early retirement. Vegas had some bittersweet memories at this point for all of them.

"I will. And we'll plan video chats every few days."

With one last goodbye, which had Lyric tearing up this time, her mom disappeared into the taxi. After closing her front door, she wandered around the empty town house. She already missed having her niece's chatter and her mom's calm, steady presence. She was now on her own with her niece for the first time in her life. And, suddenly, she wasn't sure she could do it. She knew exactly how Jacob Sellers's parents felt. That whole vibe of knowing it was the right thing but not feeling sure you were capable.

Yes, you are, Ly. You have to be. That little girl has no one else and you can't expect your mom and dad to take on raising her. Not when you have the means...and no romantic commitments to interfere.

Breaking up with Jim actually couldn't have come at a better time, as painful as it had been at the time.

Going into the little girl's room, she admired the decorating efforts of her mom and niece. Her green comforter was scattered with various throw pillows and a couple of jungle animals—a sloth and an elephant, to be exact—were there to keep Alia company. Her gaze moved to the framed picture on the dresser. She went over and picked it up. It was a picture of Tessa and Alia, when the child was barely a year old. Her sister—although rail-thin—smiled down at her daughter as if she didn't have a care in the world, when in reality she was probably thinking about her next fix.

Fortunately, Tessa had had no problem leaving Alia in her parents' care, so there'd been no court battles, just a steady attempt to help their daughter beat her habit. A fight Lyric had joined in. But nothing had seemed to work. And now she was gone.

She hugged the photo to her and closed her eyes. "I'm sorry, Tess," she whispered. "So, so sorry. But I promise I'm going to spend the rest of my life loving your daughter and doing what I can to help others like you."

The picture went back on the dresser, her fingers trailing over it one last time. She was sure that at some point Alia would ask about her mom, and they would need to have a talk about what had happened. But today was not that day. And now she needed to go get ready for her meeting with Ellis and pray that he would help her keep the promise she'd just made to her sister and Alia.

He saw her the second she arrived. Dressed in dark jeans and a cream scoop-necked shirt, she looked tall and elegant, her dark hair almost grazing her shoulders. The cut was modern and almost choppy, the different-length strands curving this way and that, giving her an air of assured independence. And it was right on target with what he knew about her. She was stubborn and determined and didn't let much stand in her way.

If she had her way, she'd probably take this project on by herself, but that wasn't smart for more than one reason. First, she was emotionally invested in the outcome, because of her sister. And second, they needed to be able to sell this to the board, and for that to happen, it needed more than one supporter.

And Ellis wasn't positive he could give her that support. If they got into the neighborhoods and he didn't think the hospital was the right entity for the fight, he was going to speak up and say so. But he'd told her he'd keep an open mind, and he would. He'd already crossed three expensive pieces of equipment off his wish list to help leave some funding open. He just didn't want to be throwing money into a black hole that benefitted no one except those in administration.

He lifted a hand to catch her attention and she nodded, going up to order her coffee. This particular coffee shop was attached to a public library and also sold chocolates from a local chocolatier. He watched her peruse the glass-fronted case, pointing to something she'd spotted. The person behind the counter quickly packaged it up and handed it to her, along with a beverage. She then made her way over to his table.

Sliding into the seat across from this, she smiled. "I love this place. I'll have to bring Alia here. She can check books out and get a hot chocolate."

He nodded at the small box. "Looks like you got a little more than hot chocolate."

"Yes, unfortunately. Turtles are a weakness

of mine. And I got a cappuccino with a shot of vanilla—not hot chocolate—to go along with it."

"Turtles?"

Up went her eyebrows. "You've never had a Turtle? Ever?"

"I take it we're not talking about a reptile."

She opened the box. "Here. Try one. It's milk chocolate with caramel and pecans. They also make them in dark chocolate with several different kinds of nuts."

He took one and waited as she also selected a chocolate. She bit into hers, a long string of caramel coming off the candy. Part of it landed on her lower lip. She chewed, her tongue darting out to sweep away the stray stickiness.

Ellis's mouth watered, the reaction having nothing to do with the candy and everything to do with what he'd just witnessed. He'd thought meeting on neutral ground had been a good idea, but now he wasn't so sure. He popped his own candy into his mouth and bit down.

She was right. It was good. The slight bitterness of the pecans blended nicely with the sweetness of the caramel and chocolate.

She paused with the rest of the candy near her pink lips. Lips that looked far softer than they should. A fleeting thought circled his skull. Would he be able to taste the caramel that had rested there moments earlier?

"Good?" she asked.

"Very." There was a little too much emphasis on that word, and he wasn't sure if it had to do with the candy itself or his ridiculous imaginings.

"I can see this is going to be a dangerous place to hang out."

Yes, it was. At least after this. She didn't mean the two of them, though. Of that, he was certain.

"Several parents of my patients have mentioned this place, and I thought it would be a good chance to check it out." Right now, he was pretty sure he should have picked a different day to do that.

"Alia will love it."

"How is she doing, by the way?" He hadn't seen the child again since that day in Lyric's office.

"Great. She loves her preschool so far. My mom went home this morning, so things will be a little more challenging than they were, but we'll manage."

"Let me know if I can help." *What? Where had that come from?* "And don't worry about being late or needing to leave early."

"Thanks. Hopefully that will be very rare, and I'll make sure it doesn't interfere with my work. I'm still looking for a sitter for the weekends or for days that the school is closed." She cleared her throat, taking a sip of her coffee and then lifting a tote bag she'd brought with her onto the table. "I brought a notebook to keep track of what we've done and the sections of town we've visited. Anything I should know?"

The next twenty minutes were spent with Ellis pulling up a map on his phone and sharing the research he'd done on the different areas. She added the work she'd done on social resources in the greater Atlanta area along with a list of rehab centers she'd found online.

It seemed they'd both come prepared. He liked that.

"So what do you think needs to happen, exactly? Where do you see holes in the system?"

"Well, in Vegas I would have loved to have schools take a trip to rehab centers, or maybe have addicts who have successfully kicked their habit mentor at-risk students. I think that might work here, as well, since I didn't see anything like that being done."

"And who would select these students? I can see a danger in it appearing to be profiling."

"I'm hoping parents will step up and recognize problems in their own households. People who want to get help for their kids before it's too late."

He could see the value in that. She really had done a lot of thinking and researching without him asking and despite having her niece to take care of. A sliver of admiration worked its way under his skin, making itself known each time she said something new.

"So can we set a date to go through these six areas?" He made a note to himself to get a dose or two of naloxone to take with them, just in case, although he hoped they didn't run into any cases of opioid overdose while they were out.

"My schedule is probably lighter than yours is right now, so if you can give me a date, I'll put it in my phone."

Glancing through his calendar, he realized she was right. He had few completely open days, except for the weekends. "Any chance you could go on a Saturday or Sunday?"

"I have Alia at home on weekends. If you map out some areas, maybe we could go at separate times and report our findings to each other."

He thought for a minute. "I'd rather try to be on the same page, if we can. It's hard to bounce around ideas by text, when we're not both experiencing the same things at the same time."

Experiencing the same things? Something about that sounded off to him, although he couldn't really put a finger on why.

She laughed. "Any chance your friend Dave has kids and could schedule a play date with Alia?"

He really didn't want her relying on Dave, and again, he wasn't sure exactly why. "He doesn't have kids. Sorry."

"Well, we're at an impasse then, it would seem. You're busy during the week, and I'm busy on weekends."

"Most of my surgeries are in the morning. I can juggle my schedule and get three or four hours over the course of a couple of afternoons. That would give us a good start. What time do you have to pick up your niece in the afternoons?"

"Preschool ends at two, but they have an after-care program that in extenuating circumstances can hold them until six. They need at least a day's notice, and I would rather not go that route every day, but periodically it would be okay."

"All right." He looked at his calendar again. "We have Jacob's parents two days from now, but how about tomorrow and then again on Friday?"

"That should work. I'll let the school know."

"Can I give you a ride back to the hospital?" The offer came out before he could stop it, but really, it was the polite thing to do.

"I drove, but thanks. I'll see you at the Sellers appointment, then, if not before." She nodded at her little box. "Would you like another for the road?"

"I'm good." He really didn't want to risk seeing her bite into another one. Especially after watching her lick the sweet center off her lips. Because as much as he might deny it to himself, he hadn't been able to stop himself from imagining kissing that bit of caramel off her. Something he was never ever going to do. Which is why it was better to not even leave the door open for thoughts like that.

He stood. "I'll see you later, then."

"Okay, sounds good." And as she opened the lid of the box and took out another chocolate, he turned on his heel and headed for the exit, and an escape that right now looked sweeter than that whole damn box of candy.

CHAPTER FIVE

LYRIC HAD NOTIFIED the preschool that she wouldn't be in to pick up Alia until sometime after four. She hoped her young niece wouldn't get worried, although she'd talked to her about it the previous evening, so she was prepared.

Waiting at the front of the hospital for Ellis, she found herself a ball of nerves all over again. What was it about this man that made her react like that?

Maybe it was the way his gaze had dipped to her mouth when she'd been eating her candy and gotten some of it on her lip. She'd gone very still, not realizing she was holding her breath until his eyes came back up to look past her.

God. Her whole body had vibrated in a way she didn't recognize. And that was scary.

As if knowing she was thinking about him, Ellis came striding down the hallway, dressed in jeans and a black polo shirt. He looked amazing, making her wish she'd brought that box of candy with her. Except she'd gone home and eaten the whole thing in almost a sitting. Just so she wouldn't have to think about what had happened anymore.

"Hi, sorry I'm late. Surgery ran a little longer than I expected."

She couldn't stop a smile. "Not a problem. I haven't been here long." Was it her imagination or was the lady in the reception booth checking out Ellis? It was the same young lady who'd been there the day she'd arrived. She hadn't noticed it then, but she'd been a nervous wreck after arriving late. "And it's good to know that I'm not the only one who can be delayed."

"Touché." He evidently didn't need to ask what she was talking about. "I thought we'd take my car, since I'm more familiar with the area."

His eyes never even strayed to the information booth, which made some of Lyric's tension slide away, although that was ridiculous.

"Good, because I'd probably get lost, even using the GPS on my phone."

Making their way to the parking lot, Ellis stopped in front of a shiny, black BMW. Her eyes went big. "This won't stand out at all. Maybe we should take the bus."

"It'll be fine. We won't be going into the worst of the worst areas, since they're the farthest away from the hospital."

She nodded and waited for him to click open the locks from a keypad on the side of the car. Sliding into the leather seat, she found herself inhaling before she realized what was happening, and tried to catch his scent in the vehicle. And she did, along with the smell of warm leather and…coffee. She spied a cup in a holder, a small curl of steam coming from the vent on the lid, obviously from a different coffee shop than the one she'd met him at yesterday. Her mouth watered, wishing she'd brought one of her own.

"I'm jealous. I didn't even think of bringing coffee."

"I brought that for you, actually. Cappuccino with a shot of vanilla, right?"

She blinked. He remembered what she drank? "Thank you. You didn't get one for yourself?"

"I had an espresso. It was quick to drink."

She picked up the cup and took a sip. "Mmm, perfect. I guess I should have brought some Turtles in trade."

"Look in the back."

She twisted around and spotted a small familiar box. She gulped as something in her tummy started tingling at the way he'd looked at her the last time they'd had Turtles.

Not the marrying kind, remember? And neither are you. Now.

But why did it have to be marriage at all?

Because she'd already done the casual-relationship thing and it hadn't been satisfying. At all. But maybe that was because she'd been expecting something deeper, when Jim had had no intention of making their pillow talk into anything permanent.

"You didn't have to get me those."

He started the car, turning to look at her with a raised eyebrow. "Oh, Lyric. Who said they were for you?"

She laughed. "They are addicting, aren't they?" As soon as the words were out of her mouth, her laughter dried up. It was crazy how she used to be able to shoot those words out like they meant nothing. "Sorry. That wasn't very funny, given the circumstances."

"Hey…" His hand touched hers, those funny callouses making themselves known again. "You have to keep some separation or it'll drive you crazy."

"And you? How are you able to keep separate from things that hurt?"

He took his hand off hers, a muscle in his jaw pulsing. "I think some people find it easier to stay emotionally detached."

Was he saying she couldn't? That stung, but she wasn't going to let him know it. She decided to change the subject.

"Can I see your hand?"

"Excuse me?"

Oh, Lord. Why had she asked that? She was supposed to be going for something less personal, not more. "Sorry. I noticed you have calluses and wondered what they were from."

And why had she noticed that in the first place? She'd shaken hands with hundreds of men and never thought twice about what their palms felt like.

Maybe he did yard work, or sailed or something.

He turned one of his hands over and glanced briefly at it as they pulled onto the interstate. "I do a little woodworking in my spare time."

"Woodworking?" It took a second for the words to compute.

"I make furniture, actually."

"Wow. I didn't know people did that much anymore."

She pictured him leaning over some piece of wood and slowly working it, his hands gliding over each inch of it, feeling the warmth and life he was breathing into the piece. A shudder rolled through her before she could stop it. Maybe it would have been better if he *had* simply raked leaves to get those calluses.

He shrugged. "Let's just say I find satisfaction in something being finished. Something that has nothing to do with sickness or death or trying to diagnose something you've never come across before."

"I can understand that."

She hadn't been searching for pieces to the puzzle that made up Ellis, but felt like she was holding a couple in her hand right now. "At least you don't have to worry about getting emotionally involved with a piece of wood."

Except she'd imagined him doing just that, hadn't she? Or was the wood merely a substitute for something very different?

Darn it, Ly! Don't go placing yourself on this man's sawhorses.

"You're right. You don't get emotionally involved."

She needed to stop this train of thought. Right now. "So where are we going first?"

"Merit. It's the neighborhood on our list that is closest to the hospital, but it's also the area with more resources. We're about five minutes away."

A mile or two later, he took an exit and turned onto a quiet street. Right away, Lyric saw graffiti on the overpass they'd just exited. But the houses didn't look as run-down as she'd expected. "Are we there?"

"Yes. We're headed to a high school that has a reputation for drug use."

Another turn, and she spotted a large brick building with sign out front saying it was the Merit high school. They drove by at a fairly slow rate, noticing a police presence on two of the neighboring streets, along with a lot of other parked cars.

"Looks like maybe they're working to combat the problem, too."

"I would say that's the case, as well," he said. "I don't want to cruise by more than once or we'll look suspicious. Let's move a little farther out on the grid."

Just then, students started pouring from the

entrance like a hose that had suddenly been turned on full blast, and the school-zone light started blinking.

Two of the kids that passed them lit up cigarettes as soon as they were across the street, despite the police presence. Several others followed suit.

"Hell, why do they do that to themselves at that age?"

She understood exactly what he meant. Lyric had found Tessa smoking on more than one occasion when she was in middle school. Besides being illegal, Lyric had found that it became easy to swap one addiction for another, since they all caused dopamine levels to rise, rewarding the user with that feeling of being normal and happy. But the younger they started, the more they wanted to recapture that feeling and hold onto it. Lyric was convinced that smoking had started the ball rolling with Tessa. Maybe it didn't with everyone, but there was a connection with addiction and genetics. Maybe Tessa had inherited something and smoking flipped a switch in her brain that opened the door and transformed something from taboo to "normal."

The police weren't doing anything, but then again, they were probably looking for something much worse, like dealers. They left the school zone and did a slow circle, eventually going farther and farther away.

"Hey, there's a rehab facility. And it's not very far from the school, either."

"There are several in the area from what I saw online."

"I guess we could contact them and see if they have any kind of programs to help mentor school-aged kids. I almost feel like we need to start at the middle-school level, or maybe even younger."

She jotted down the name of the rehab center, making a note to give them a call later on today. They passed a group of about ten kids who were standing in a tight circle. "That's weird. Wonder what they're doing?"

There were no police on this block and a shiver went through her. Someone had his

phone out, held way up high like he was film-
ing something. A fight? No, she didn't see
any commotion going on. She turned her
head as they went by, still trying to figure out
what was bothering her. She suddenly saw a
ripple of activity. Then she realized someone
had emerged from the group and was yelling
for help. Screaming, actually.

"Stop, Ellis! Something's wrong."

He pulled over immediately, maneuvering
between two parked cars. Someone sprinted
from the scene. This person was older. Slick-
looking. She didn't like it.

She was out of the car in a flash, rushing
toward the group, even as Ellis popped his
trunk and took out what looked like a medical bag.

"What's going on?" she asked the nearest
person.

"Who are you?" A belligerent teen blocked
her path.

"I'm a doctor. Is someone hurt?"

A girl ran over to her and grabbed her arm.

"A man was trying to show her how, and she suddenly fell over."

"Trying to show her how to what?"

Scared eyes stared into hers. "How to find a vein."

Oh, God. A million thoughts went through her head. Had the person actually injected her with anything? Pushed in an air bubble? "What was in the hypo?"

"I don't want to get her in trouble." By now the crowd of kids realized an adult was on the scene and scattered faster than she would have believed possible, leaving the girl she was talking to and another girl on the ground. Two other girls stood back, gripping each other. They looked no older than fourteen. Her sister's face swam before her eyes.

"I need you to tell me. Her life depends on it." Holding on to the girl, she dragged her to the victim just as Ellis reached them.

He motioned to one of the two girls who were watching. "Call 911." When neither of them moved, he raised his voice and pointed at one of them. "Do it! Now!"

The girl nearest to him pulled out her phone and dialed.

"She's not breathing," Ellis said. "Start CPR."

The girl she was holding moaned. "No, Alisha! Oh, my God." She looked Lyric in the eye. "It was heroin. Please help her."

Getting on the ground beside the stricken girl, Lyric found the spot in her chest and began compressions. "We need naloxone."

Ellis was already in his bag just as she heard sirens, but she kept counting down the number of compressions. He came over with a needle of his own. "I've got it. Stop compressions for a second."

Swabbing her arm with alcohol, he injected the life-saving medicine while Lyric started compressions again. Ellis fitted a manual breathing device over the girl's mouth. Lyric stopped so he could pump a couple of breaths and then started back up. "One, two, three, four, five, six…"

They should know in just a few minutes if it was effective.

A uniformed officer hurried over to them, and Ellis quickly explained who they were, telling the man they'd administered naloxone.

Just then the sound of a ragged breath came from the girl on the ground. She turned her head and vomited.

"EMS is on their way," the officer said.

The girl who had called 911 was long gone, but the friend of the downed girl was still there sobbing. He turned to her. "I need her name and an emergency contact number."

"She's my sister..." She sobbed wildly. "She's not going to die, is she?"

Shock roared through Lyric and a sense of déjà vu almost overcame her. She'd assumed the other girl was just a friend. She swallowed, trying to keep her mind on her patient.

Ellis was next to her, checking pupillary reactions and taking her pulse. She glanced at the girl standing over them. "Are you using, too?"

"She's my baby sister."

Lyric bit her tongue as a million ugly words came to mind. She'd done everything in her power to help Tessa kick her habit and to find an older sister actually helping the younger one to follow in her footsteps… She couldn't begin to understand that mind-set.

"Are. You. Using?" She made her voice hard.

"Not for very long." She looked at Lyric through brown tearstained eyes.

"Listen to me. Your sister could have died. If we hadn't gotten here when we did, she would have. Is that what you want?"

She shook her head, but didn't say anything.

The officer put his hand on the girl's arm. "She's right. Your sister is very lucky. We're going to call your parents, and then we're all going to sit down and have a long talk, okay?"

"Y-yes."

EMS got there and took over care, writing down the information from Ellis's syringe. "Lucky you were on the scene."

Ellis looked at Lyric and nodded. "It looks that way. I don't normally carry naloxone with me, but since we were doing research in this area for the hospital, I decided to bring a couple of doses, just in case we ran into something."

She hadn't even thought of bringing any. Then again, she hadn't expected to find someone OD'ing on the street.

But Ellis had come prepared. His speech about staying emotionally detached came back to her. Maybe she really did have a problem.

"An older male ran from the scene, while another person filmed the situation on his phone," he said to the officer. "You might want to see if you can find the person, if you need a visual when you investigate."

"We'll do that. Thanks."

She remembered seeing someone with the phone pointed toward the scene, too. What kind of sick individual recorded someone who might be dying?

Had someone filmed Tessa's last fix?

As soon as the girl and her sister were loaded into the ambulance and the sirens faded away, Lyric stood on the sidewalk shaking, arms wrapped around her waist, while Ellis finished giving the police officer a statement. God. She hoped he didn't need her to do the same, because she was going to come apart, if so.

She sucked down one deep breath and then another, and prayed she could make it home before she made a total fool of herself in front of Ellis and whoever else happened by.

Ellis glanced over at Lyric after the officer had him sign his statement. Something didn't look right. She looked totally alone standing on the sidewalk, and her eyes…

Stricken. He'd seen that same expression on the face of parents who'd been told there was no hope for survival for their child. But the girl from today had survived. And maybe she and her sister had both gotten the wake-up call they needed. Lyric should be relieved they'd happened across the scene. And yet there was no evidence of that on her face.

"Do you need anything else?"

"No, sir, we'll contact you if we do. Thanks again for stepping in to help."

"It's part of my job."

Yes, it was. So why did this feel like something else? At least on Lyric's side.

He walked over to where she was standing. "You okay?"

"Yeah, fine." She even nodded as if she needed to emphasize that fact.

"I'm beginning to think you're right about the need for some mentors or something. Today never should have happened."

"No. It shouldn't have."

He frowned. He was right. There was something going on with her. "Let's get back to the car."

"Can we just walk for a few minutes? I need some air."

The air was pretty warm and humid this time of year, but he nodded. "Sure. Let me just put my bag away and lock the car."

"Oh, I'm sorry. I'm sure you need to get back to the hospital."

"I'm good." He glanced at her for a minute. "Tell you what. There's a park not too far from here—it's a quick drive. Why don't we go there? We can save the rest of the locations for another time or Friday, like we talked about."

"Thank you. That sounds wonderful."

He stowed his medical gear and they climbed in the vehicle. Less than fifteen minutes later, they were at one of the smaller parks that dotted Atlanta's scenery. The entire way, Lyric had been silent. Maybe it was the crash after the rush of adrenaline from administering CPR.

"This is beautiful." She climbed out and looked around at the greenery.

"It is. Some of the five-Ks I've participated in have been in this park."

"I can see why."

He tried looking at the area as if seeing it for the first time. A paved path meandered through patches of trees and grassy areas, a solid white line dividing it in two. Park benches were planted along the way at regular intervals.

He knew from coming here that there was also a dirt running path with hills and planned uneven areas for those who wanted a more strenuous workout. The park was popular because of the various activities it offered, as well as distance markers that helped keep track of how far you'd gone. Even now a few runners passed by, despite the heat of the afternoon sun.

They entered through the gates, and a sign informed them that the area was patrolled on a regular basis. Lyric nodded at it. "I'm glad to see that."

"I should have warned you that some of the areas we'll be visiting are rough. Sorry you had to see it on your first trip."

She stopped and looked at him, blinking. "You think I was scared?"

He thought through his words carefully. "No, I think it was an emotionally charged situation and adrenaline—"

"Adrenaline had nothing to do with it." Her flat tone held a warning.

"What then?" He was trying to understand, but somehow failed to grasp what she meant.

"My sister OD'd. I've often wondered if she could have survived had someone in the vicinity had a dose of naloxone." Her lips twisted. "And yet, I never even thought to bring some with us."

"Hey, I almost didn't, either. It was sheer luck that I packed it."

She took a step closer, her expression softening. "Ellis, you saved that girl's life."

He swallowed, looking into eyes that were moist with emotion. Some answering sentiment appeared out of nowhere, the sensation odd and unfamiliar. And yet it felt right. Sliding a finger under her chin, he tilted her head. "So did you. You kept her alive until the naloxone could take effect."

"I felt totally paralyzed, as if I were experiencing my sister's situation firsthand. I was scared we weren't in time. And when she took that first breath, God…" Her chest rose, as if mimicking what the girl had done. "I thought I was going to fall to pieces."

"But you didn't."

"You have no idea how close I was."

"She's alive. That's all that matters." He cupped her face, noting how exquisite her bone structure was as he brushed a bead of moisture from beneath her eye. "I'm sorry it couldn't be the same for your sister."

"What happened to staying emotionally detached?" Her smile was shaky. "Looks like you're not always as gruff as you appear."

"Gruff, huh?" He smiled. "I've been called a lot of things, some not very nice, but I think that's the first time I've been called that. At least to my face."

His gaze trailed to her lips, watching as her teeth caught at the lower one in a way that made things tighten. He remembered the caramel from the coffee shop. How he'd thought about kissing it. Kissing her.

"Maybe it's because of how you were the day we met."

He had been kind of a bear that day. But his mood was more from hearing that the grant money his department had been promised might have to be shared for something that wasn't on his list. But he was beginning to think maybe it should have been. That girl from today had probably been transported to New Mercy, and someone from Pediatrics was almost assuredly going to be called on to help with her care.

"I'm surprised you didn't call me a stronger word than that."

"How do you know I didn't?"

His smile widened. "In that case, I won't ask." The tips of her hair brushed across his fingers, feeling silky soft, her skin warm despite having just left an air-conditioned car.

"Maybe Dr. Lawson was right. Your bark was worse than your bite."

"Don't be too sure about that."

Suddenly he knew his crazy fantasies were going to come to fruition. He was going to kiss her. The combination of their back-and-forth banter and having her so close were doing a number on him, and he was finding it harder and harder to resist.

If he was going to back away, he needed to do so now.

He stayed rooted in place instead.

"Lyric?"

"Mmm?"

She looked relaxed and comfortable, whereas moments earlier she'd said she'd been at a breaking point. He wasn't sure if he'd made the difference or if it was just the passing of time. But it was also the first time he could remember her not looking like she was on edge, waiting for something to happen.

He liked it. Wanted to keep this version of Lyric around for a while.

And so he did what he'd been wanting to do for the last half hour. He leaned down and kissed her.

CHAPTER SIX

THE SECOND HIS mouth touched hers, Lyric felt the earth shift under her feet.

His lips were warm and firm, just like she'd imagined they'd be. And, yes, she had imagined them. Time and time again, despite the numerous cease-and-desist warnings she'd sent to her brain.

Her efforts had failed and now she knew. And the kiss was every bit as heady as the stray images she'd intercepted inside her head.

Not good. Because she didn't want to like the kiss. She should shove him away and ask him what he thought he was doing. But she didn't. Because she was a very willing participant in what was happening. In fact, she didn't want it to stop…wanted it to keep on going for ages.

Her arms crept up and rounded his neck, as if she was afraid he might suddenly pull away. But, so far, he was showing no signs of moving.

Something whizzed by them, a bicycle, probably, but she didn't care, didn't stop to make sure they were out of the way of passersby.

He shifted his angle and the thought ran through her head that even his kiss was gruff. As if it had taken him by surprise, and he hadn't been able to stop himself. His teeth nipped at her bottom lip, making her edge even closer, the languid warmth in her tummy changing to something that churned with heat. And need.

She was pretty sure he'd started off with the intention of comforting her. And she'd wanted the comfort. Until the word *more* whispered through her head. She'd needed more, and it was almost as if he'd heard her thoughts and was giving her what she wanted.

Her fingers slid into his hair and found it

warm and crisp, a muffled groan coming from him when she explored deeper.

A giggle sounded nearby, and she realized it hadn't come from her. Or from him.

That made her pull free with a gulp. Ellis was just as quick to let her go. Her eyes searched the area and saw a couple walking side by side, hands clasped. The girl glanced back at them with a knowing smile.

Oh, Lord. Did the woman think Ellis was her boyfriend? Her lover?

He was neither.

A flash of panic came over her. She had Alia to think about. And all his talk of emotional detachment came back in a rush.

What had she been thinking? She stepped back in a hurry. "I'm so sorry. You were right. After the adrenaline and everything..." She waved her hand around as if she could grab the rest of the explanation out of thin air. She found nothing. Except worry. Worry that she would ruin everything, and he would send her packing. Worry that her first week with

Alia would be overshadowed with thinking about what had happened.

"I'm the one who should be sorry. You were upset. And I knew better."

She blinked. "You didn't do it on purpose."

"No. Of course not. But I sensed you weren't yourself. I never should have kissed you."

"I'd like to think we both got caught up in the moment." It was the truth. Because once his hands cradled her face, she was a goner. If he hadn't initiated that kiss, she almost certainly would have. So she was really as much, if not more, to blame for what happened as he was.

She continued, "Well, at least we both realize it was a mistake." It had been, hadn't it? Or was she making too big of a deal about it?

"I don't make a habit of kissing coworkers. And it won't happen again."

Was he worried she would go to HR and report him? Not very likely. She didn't want anyone to know what had happened. And he really hadn't done anything wrong. Neither had she.

So why did she feel guilty?

Because she had a young niece who needed her right now. And one thing Alia didn't need was the confusion of seeing her aunt kiss someone and wonder if that "someone" was going to be a fixture in their lives. Thank God she'd broken things off with Jim. Although she almost certainly would have once Alia became her responsibility.

And she was not going to repeat her mistakes with someone else.

"I'm sure you don't. Neither do I. So I vote that we forget about it."

"Forget about it. Sure."

There was an odd note to his voice, but if she had to guess what he was feeling, she would say relief. Because that's what she was feeling. Right?

Of course.

"Do you still want to be there when I meet with Jacob Sellers's parents?"

"Yes, unless you think that would be a distraction."

It would, but she didn't want him to know

that. And by the time that appointment rolled around, her feet would be back on terra firma and today would be just a faint memory.

"Of course not. Besides, we agreed to forget about what happened."

"Sounds good. Let's get back to the hospital. I'd like to check on the girl who OD'd and see how she's doing."

"Could you call me and let me know once you find out?" Right now she needed to get away from him. Because the longer she stood in this park and looked at him, the less likely she'd be to keep her resolution of putting this behind her. Because even now, there was a voice at the back of her head that whispered, *That resolution begins tomorrow, right? Not today. So why not just have that one last little binge before the fasting begins?*

Fasting? Ugh. This was more than just going on a diet. This was a knife slice that separated what had happened today from what would happen in the future.

"I will."

So they made the trek back to the car in silence, for the most part. However, Lyric was painfully aware of everything about him as they walked and as they drove back to the hospital. And that did not bode well for putting this behind her. But somehow she had to. For her sake. And for Alia's. The little girl did not need any more turmoil in her young life. Lyric had to put her own wants and needs on the back burner for a while. No matter how hard that might prove.

Ellis stood outside of the door to Lyric's office two days later. The overdose victim had survived, much to everyone's relief, and both the girl and her sister were now getting the counseling they needed to hopefully prevent this from happening again. He'd debated a couple of times since then about pulling back from the Jacob Sellers case, but knew if it wasn't that situation, there would be others that would require him to work with Lyric.

He'd beat himself up several times over the past couple of days. He wasn't quite sure what had happened. He'd seen grief before.

Many times, in fact, but he'd never allowed any emotion to come between him and his objectivity.

Maybe it was the fact that those emotions had even arisen that had caused this. Ellis normally had to work on summoning some semblance of compassion, so it was the fact that this had seemingly erupted out of nowhere that had shocked him and made him act impulsively.

And he didn't like it. He preferred his old style of dealing with things, even if it did earn him adjectives like *hard-nosed* or *emotionless* from some of the staff.

There was nothing to do but knock on the door and face her. It had to happen sometime. Maybe he shouldn't have worked so hard on making sure their paths didn't cross. Because this was not the best setting for making that first contact.

He almost groaned aloud as the thought made the memory of another "first contact" arise.

Forcing his knuckles to strike the surface

of her door, he rapped twice, hearing her call out for him to enter. When he did, he found the Sellerses already in the room and Lyric holding an orange.

On the computer screen that faced the couple was a diagram with various subcutaneous injection sites circled.

He greeted the couple and asked how Jacob was doing.

"He's been asking when he can start getting his 'growing medicine.'"

Lyric smiled. "That's a good sign. I really think he's going to do just fine."

Ellis wondered why she hadn't brought in one of the practice mannequins, although he knew the old standard was an orange. He glanced at his phone, thinking maybe he was late, but he wasn't. It was still five minutes before their meeting time. He tried not to be irritated that she'd started without him, but recognized that it didn't make sense for her to just sit there with the couple without actively doing what they'd come there for.

She obviously didn't always run late, like she had that first day.

"So as I was saying," she said, pointing to the areas on the screen. "Any of these sites are fine, and we already talked about rotating where you give the injections."

She handed an injection pen to Mrs. Sellers, while she held the orange. "Since you said you'll probably be doing the majority of the injections because of work schedules, we'll start with you. Do it just like I showed you."

Mrs. Sellers did great setting up the needle and dialing in the amount of growth hormone. But when she got to the part where she had to push the plunger, she hesitated. "You're sure it won't hurt?"

"It's best to just push it with purpose. He'll barely feel it. A good option would be to wait for him to go to sleep, as I mentioned last time we met."

He was impressed with how matter-of-fact and confident Lyric was. And that confidence seemed to transfer to the husband and wife as they both succeeded with their practice injections.

Soon they were done and out of the room.

"That went well." He watched her clear away the items they'd used, putting the trash in one receptacle and the needle in the portable sharps box she'd brought into her office. "We do have a practice mannequin, if you want to use it."

"We might next time, but I wanted them to become familiar with the pen itself without having to worry about where exactly to give the injection. 'One skill at a time' was one of my instructor's mottos. I've tended to find that to be true."

It made sense. He glanced at her to see if there was any hint of being uncomfortable around him. "I saw you started early."

"I did. Sorry. They were in the waiting room, and I was done with the patient I'd been speaking with. I thought we'd just get started. I hope that was okay."

"Of course. How's your niece doing with her new preschool?"

Lyric made a quick face. "Not as well as I'd hoped. She's started crying every day when I leave, although she's fine when I go to pick her up."

"Are you bringing her here after preschool is over?"

"I have been, only because I'd rather not bombard her with having to switch from one day-care setting to another on top of the move and everything else. I hope that's not a problem."

"Not at all. I was the one who suggested it." He softened the words with a smile, hoping they hadn't come across as condescending.

Only now did he notice that she had slight smudges under her eyes...and she only had on one earring. A testament to how hard a time she was having adjusting? An unfamiliar pang went through him at the thought that she might throw in the towel and go back to Vegas. "Did you lose a...?" He motioned to his own ear.

She reached up and touched one lobe

and then the other, the action sending a jolt through his chest.

Then she rolled her eyes. "Oh, God. It's just been one of those days." She smiled back. "You know, when nothing goes according to plan?"

He did indeed. He'd had one of those two days ago, when his trip to one of the project sites had gone spinning out of his control. He certainly hadn't planned on kissing her. Or reviving a child who'd overdosed. "Yes, I do. Those days are never fun."

Well, that wasn't strictly true. The kiss had been pretty awesome, although that made it dangerous, not fun.

Lyric undid the tiny diamond in her other ear and dropped it into her desk drawer. "Thanks for noticing. Hopefully no one else has."

Why *had* he noticed it? Maybe because he was used to seeing her twirl those little dots when she was uncomfortable. Or maybe it was just boredom. But today she hadn't even tried. Did that mean she was becoming more comfortable with the hospital? With him?

Doubtful. Because he was still just as on edge around her. Maybe even more than he'd been before.

All because of that damn kiss.

Today she wore a black scoop-necked blouse and cream trousers that hugged her hips just enough to bring his attention to them.

Or maybe that was just his mind roaming through areas that he'd marked as restricted territory.

She set the orange on her desk. He glanced at it with a frown. "Are you going to eat that?"

"I was. The pen was a dummy, so no actual serum was injected and the needle was sterile. I don't like to waste food."

He grinned. That was such a Lyric thing to say. And how had he even known that? Or that she'd managed to make him smile when he wasn't feeling particularly cheerful? "I hope that's not your actual lunch."

"No. I'll grab something on my way to pick

up Alia." She bit the corner of her lip. "Can I ask you something?"

He tensed but held onto his smile. "Sure."

"If I'm ever busy with a patient during the time I need to pick her up, do you know of anyone at the hospital who is trustworthy and who would be willing to be added to the approved pick-up list at the school? I don't have any relatives here, and don't really know anyone all that well yet. They could just bring her here to the hospital."

Before he even had a chance to entertain other possibilities, he heard words emerge from his mouth that had no chance of being retracted. "I can, if you think it will help. Most of my surgeries are in the morning and surely we won't both be tied up with patients at the same time."

She frowned. "Are you sure? It won't be forever. I'm hoping she'll settle into a routine and will eventually be able to be enrolled in an after-care program. Just right now I can't see my way to—"

"It's fine. I don't mind." It really wasn't

fine, but he'd already said the words and couldn't really take them back. "What do I need to do?"

"I'll need you go to with me to the preschool so they can get a picture of you to put in their files along with your signature—and mine, of course. So if we could set a day and time to do that—"

"I'm free now, and—" he nodded at the orange "—I haven't had lunch, either, so why don't we grab that bite on the way. Or do you have another patient to see right now?"

"No, the Sellerses were my last scheduled patients. But I do have paperwork to catch up on this afternoon, so I thought I'd bring Alia back here and let her play on the floor while I work."

"Good. Do you need to wrap up anything before we go? You said she gets off at two, right?" It was almost twelve thirty now.

"She does get off at two." She hesitated. "Are you sure? I wasn't hinting for you to volunteer, I honestly was just looking for suggestions. I just haven't had time to make many friends yet…" Her voice trailed away, as if she was embarrassed by that fact. "It takes me a while. Lucky you—you're the only person I really know here."

A sliver of awareness went through him. She only knew him?

It meant nothing. He'd been at this hospital for years and could still count the number of friendships on one hand. Dave Butler was one of the few people in his life that he would consider a close friend. It wasn't that he spurned friendships so much as valued his work above those kinds of relationships. It was where he felt the most comfortable.

And the fact that he'd impulsively kissed Lyric? It was not like him at all, and the warning was clear: he needed to be careful.

"I'm sure you'll make friends once you get a routine down. And it's not like I'll be picking her up every day. It might happen, what… once?"

"I hope not even that. But the preschool really wants an alternate in case of emergencies, such as if school is released early because of bad weather or other unforeseen circumstances."

"I can understand that. Not that we get much snow here. But when we do, it pretty much qualifies as a natural disaster within some government offices."

She laughed. "Good to know. Vegas is like that, too. It does snow every couple of years, but it rarely sticks."

"Anything special I should know about Alia? Will she be afraid of a stranger picking her up? Should I be around her a time or two—with you there, of course—so she gets used to me?"

"I hadn't thought about that. She has been a little weepy, recently. I don't want you to end up with a wailer on your hands."

"Wailer?" He felt even less sure about his suggestion now.

"Sorry, I'm kidding. And I really don't want to impose on you. But if you'll go with me today, so she can see you again and maybe interact with you a bit, that would be helpful.

You're a pediatrician, so it's not like it'll be a stretch for you to talk to a kid."

He was a pediatrician, but that didn't mean it wouldn't be a stretch. At the hospital, he had a goal to work toward. But with Alia...?

Wait. Maybe he could approach it like he did the kids at work. Treat this as a problem that needed a solution. Lyric's niece needed someone reliable who would be there in the event that her aunt couldn't. The goal would be to help her feel safe.

The snatches of memories he had from when his mother left were of abject terror and a sick certainty that the same men who'd taken his mom were eventually going to come and take him or Maddie away. And he would be left completely alone. No child should have to experience that, so if he could help Alia feel safe and secure—even in this small way—he was going to try.

Otherwise she might contact Dave and ask him to do it.

Where had that come from? Maybe because Dave had actually called a few days ago and asked if it would be inappropriate for him to ask her out. Ellis had had no choice but to say he had no opinion one way or the other—which wasn't entirely the case. And he had no idea why.

The image of her unhooking that earring swung around to haunt him again. And if Dave plucked those tiny studs out of her ears?

A queasy feeling roiled around inside of him.

Lyric hadn't mentioned having plans with anyone. And during that kiss he'd shared with her, she had definitely been kissing him back. Which had been part of the reason he hadn't come to his senses and pulled back sooner. Because the way she'd kissed...

Hell! No thinking about that.

Surely if she'd had a date with someone else, she would have said so afterward.

He realized she was looking at him. Waiting for him to respond to whatever she'd said. "I'm not sure about it not being a stretch, but I'll certainly do my best not to traumatize her."

"Traumatize her?" She cocked her head. "How would you do that?"

He'd meant it as a joke, but maybe subconsciously his thoughts about his own childhood had translated themselves into the conversation. He made something up. "By telling her 'Dad jokes.'"

"Don't you have to be a dad to do that?" Her features had relaxed. Surely she didn't think he would actually say something to scare her. Then again, despite her words, she didn't really know him. And if she did, maybe she wouldn't be so quick to agree to his name being on that list of alternates.

"Hmm…you've never heard any of my jokes."

"I can't picture you actually delivering a punchline. To anything." She laughed again, the light sound again pulling at something inside of him. Her brown eyes sparkled, and she tossed her head, sending strands of glossy hair flying in all directions.

It was probably the most carefree he'd seen her since she'd started working at New Mercy.

He liked it. A little belatedly, he realized he was still in her office, and the door closed. And she was standing not five feet away from him, while snatches of internal conversation were starting to make themselves heard in his head. And what they included would definitely not be on their lunch menu.

"We'd better go or that bite to eat will be smaller than my appetite."

Especially since his appetite was starting to expand into other areas. And that bothered him. A lot. His relationships with women—like the rest of his life—were things that were arranged with almost clinical precision. They didn't just "happen."

She hesitated. "If you're sure."

"I wouldn't have offered if I wasn't."

The words were a little shorter than he meant them to be. But this was real. There was no going back now—not without an awkward explanation that he'd rather not give. He repeated the argument that his signature on a piece of paper would not likely come to anything, and this would all be just an empty exercise. At least he hoped so. Because having his picture on a file that gave him responsibility over a young child...

He sucked down a quick breath. He'd assumed he'd never have anything but a medical responsibility for anyone. Especially a kid who had undergone a trauma similar to his own. Well, he was not going to screw this up.

"Okay, thanks again." She came forward and touched his hand, her fingers light, before she moved past him to the door. "It's a relief not to have to worry about that."

She might not be. But he was, now. But he would go, and in doing so put Lyric's mind at ease about her young niece. And maybe he could prevent the child from experiencing the fear of abandonment that he'd once felt. That alone made his offer worth it. And since he and the endocrinologist would be working closely together, it would prevent there being any hard feelings at this short juncture in their working relationship.

Because he was pretty sure, there would be plenty of other chances for that to happen. Especially if he couldn't get his heart back in line with what he knew to be true: that Lyric and Alia were not permanent fixtures in his life. And they never would be.

CHAPTER SEVEN

LYRIC SAT ACROSS from him at an Italian eatery that was within a ten-minute drive from Alia's preschool. She'd been so worried about that kiss turning things between them into an untenable situation, but it didn't seem to have. Unlike her, Ellis had evidently brushed it off as insignificant, at least from his attitude. She wasn't sure whether to be insulted or relieved.

Relieved. This is not a situation, like with Jim, where you wanted it to mean more than it did.

In this case, she definitely did not want it to mean anything.

"I met with Dr. Radner, and she wants us to work some cases together. I guess I should have run that past you first," she said.

Dr. Theresa Radner was one of the psychiatrists at the hospital, so it would be natural for them to collaborate on some of the cases involving children.

"No need to run it by me. Maybe talk to Jack about it, just to see if that meshes with the rest of the needs of the hospital."

He said it as if it didn't matter, but there was the slightest hardening to his tone that made her wary.

"You don't sound thrilled by the idea."

"I don't really have any thoughts about it at all. I see where you're coming from, though."

No change in his voice.

Now she was sorry she'd brought it up. Would he change his mind about being Alia's alternate for pickup? Well, if it took something as little as that to change his mind, maybe it would be better if he wasn't on the list at all. "If you're worried about it interfering with my work in Pediatrics, it won't. But since the behavioral aspect of my degree is important to me, I think the other behavioral departments should be able to call and ask for a consult, don't you?"

"I do. And like I said, it's not my decision. Ultimately, it's Jack's."

So was he saying that Jack might be the one with the problem? Because that's not what it sounded like to her. "Do you think he'll object?"

Ellis stared at her for a second as if he was going to refuse to answer. Then finally, he said, "I doubt it. The two departments have just had different focuses, that's all."

"Aren't both focused on helping children?"

"Of course." He took a bite of his ravioli and glanced over her shoulder, avoiding meeting her gaze.

Despite his words, she was feeling more and more like he was the one with the problem. And she couldn't for the life of her guess why that might be.

So she followed his example and ate for a minute or two before trying again. "I also thought she—specifically—might have some thoughts on my project. I'm still at the brainstorming stage of how things might work."

"I get that. And you don't have to justify your reasons. I'm sure it will be fine."

"Okay, that's great." It wasn't really, but what else was she going to say? She really needed to tread carefully and not forget that she was the new kid on the block.

The waitress came over and asked how the check was going to be divided. Before she could say anything, Ellis said it would be all together. When the woman left, he added, "I'm putting it on the expense account, since we've spent almost the whole meal talking business."

"I'm sorry. That was my fault. I'm sure the last thing you want to talk about is work while on your lunch break."

"I like my job." He shrugged. "It's the most important thing in my life, and I don't see that changing anytime soon."

Almost exactly what Dave had said about him. But surely he wanted to get married eventually. Although Dave said that wasn't the case.

None of her business. As long as he didn't

stand in the way of her goal, she would stay out of his personal life.

And that kiss?

That wasn't delving into his personal life. In fact, she hadn't learned very much personal about the man at all, other than that he was a great kisser. But he already knew a lot about her. Much more than she shared with most people. And that made their professional relationship pretty lopsided. But she didn't have a choice.

Or did she?

"I can tell you like your job. Did you always want to be a doctor?" So much for not asking anything personal. Except people asked that question all the time. It didn't mean she was trying to pick the padlocks on his personal life.

"Not always. I was just good at the sciences in school and seemed a natural fit."

An odd answer. Most people went into that line of work because they wanted to help people, not because they were good at science. But it wasn't like there was a right or wrong answer to that kind of a question. "And pediatrics?"

This time he hesitated. "I think I wanted kids to have a good start in life and this was one way I could help with that."

There was a conviction in his voice that hadn't been there when she'd asked her first question. It seemed like instead of getting to know him better, each revelation made him even more enigmatic than he already was.

The waitress brought back their check and Ellis signed for the meal. She was surprised to see that over an hour had gone by since they'd arrived. Alia would need to be picked up in just fifteen minutes.

"I've been keeping track, don't worry."

Had he read her mind? Because she doubted he was talking about the tab. "Thanks."

What else could she say?

A few minutes later they were at the school and asking how to add someone to the pickup list. Once the forms were filled out, the director pulled out a small digital camera and took Ellis's picture. Lyric cringed at the uneasy look on his face.

This all felt a lot more official than she thought it would. As if she was signing over Alia's care to someone else. She wasn't. At least not permanently. And her mom was on the list, too, and had gone through the exact same steps. But it hadn't seemed weird then. Not like now.

She glanced at Ellis, suddenly feeling like she was making a terrible mistake, like she'd just opened her life to someone again. Which was ridiculous. She hadn't. She would have asked any number of people in Vegas to do the same.

But those people were her friends, and Ellis was...

An acquaintance. One she'd kissed. One she might have done more with had they not been in a park or interrupted. But it would have been a one-time thing. Something that didn't really mean anything to her emotionally.

And that kind of terrified her. Is that how Jim had seen her?

Evidently, since when she asked where he saw their relationship in five years, the surprised widening of his eyes had said everything. He hadn't seen them anywhere, and certainly not married.

The school administrator thanked them for coming. As if she now saw them as a couple. Lyric wanted to set her straight, but not in front of Ellis. Maybe she could explain that they were just friends later on.

Even though they weren't friends. Not really.

He followed her as she walked toward the door of Alia's classroom. The bottom half of the Dutch door was closed, but the upper part was open, allowing a clear view of what was going on inside the room. The children were bent over some kind of project on their desks. They were drawing. No chaos, no crying. It looked like everything was being done in an orderly manner.

She breathed a sigh of relief, feeling for the first time like she'd made the right decision after loads of self-doubt.

And the decision about Ellis? Well, that wasn't so cut-and-dried.

Alia's teacher came over, looking impossibly young with her blond hair pulled back in a ponytail and a smock over her clothes. Her aide continued to help the children.

"Hi. She's doing great today. Very little crying."

Lyric clasped her hands in front of her. "I am so glad to hear that." Alia had not even looked up at the door. Instead the tiniest tip of her tongue stuck out in concentration. A huge wave of love washed over her. This child was hers to raise. To protect. To cherish. And she was going to do it for all she was worth.

I'm trying, Tessa. Believe me, I'm trying.

And part of that trying was making sure she kept her priorities straight.

"Let me see if I can tear her away from her artwork."

"What are they drawing?"

Her teacher smiled. "Something they wish for."

Lyric kept her own smile plastered on her

face, although a quiver went through her. Was Alia aware enough to have drawn a picture of her mother and wish she was with her and not an aunt? Or was she wishing for a father of her own?

She squelched the urge to look at the man next to her.

Ridiculous. She'd probably drawn a picture of a tree or beach or something. She glanced back to see that Ellis was still behind her. She'd half expected him to turn around and stride in the other direction. Probably the last thing he'd wanted was to get involved with someone who'd taken on her sister's child and promised to raise her.

Well, that was okay, because he *wasn't* involved with her. He was simply a name to put on a required piece of paper. An emergency fill-in.

Kind of like Lyric was? Her heart cramped. She had to stop thinking like that. She loved her niece and would do anything for her.

A minute later, Alia had her backpack on

and came running toward the door, a sheet of paper flapping in her tiny hand.

"Auntie Lyrie! I drew a picture for you."

The teacher opened the door, and at the last second, Lyric remembered she needed to introduce Ellis to her, just in case. "Ms. Taylor, this is Ellis Rohal, he is on my emergency contact list. If I'm ever stuck at work, he has my permission to pick Alia up from school."

Ms. Taylor stuck out her hand. "Nice to meet you. Alia is a special child."

"Nice to meet you, as well."

She was sure he didn't know how to respond to the other part of the teacher's greeting. She realized the enormity of what he'd agreed to do.

Lyric knelt down and hugged her niece, glancing at the paper she was holding out to her. "What's this?"

"It's my new kitten. I wished for her."

Relief and dismay both shot through her system. Relief that the picture was not of Tessa and dismay in that Alia was used to having a dog for company at her mom's house. She hadn't even thought about her wanting a pet here. "Your kitten?"

"Do you like her?"

Lyric forced her gaze to the drawn image on the paper. An all-black shape that might have been a kitten was in front of a girl's stick-figure legs. Alia, probably. And holding Alia's hand was a much taller figure with short dark hair and a skirt. Her heart underwent several more layers of pain. Her sister was a blond, like Alia's teacher. And her mom was gray. So that meant the person in the picture was…her.

Oh, God. Her eyes moistened to a dangerous level, threatening to spill over before she caught hold of herself and forced back the tide.

"I do like her." She stood and turned to Ellis. "Alia, this is a friend of mine—his name is Ellis. You met him once before at my office. He's going to pick you up if I ever can't."

Ellis held out his hand. "Very nice to meet you officially, Alia."

Putting her tiny hand in Ellis's much bigger one, she gave it a careful shake. "Do you have a kitty?"

He shook his head. "I don't, I'm sorry."

"It's okay. I'm getting one. You can come visit her."

Ellis shot her a quizzical look. "I'll have to ask Auntie Lyrie if it's okay."

Hearing him say her name like Alia did made Lyric's chest tighten.

"It's okay, right, Auntie Lyrie?"

"O-of course." Too late, she realized the question had been in reference to him coming to meet her kitten. "But we'll have to see about the kitten. I would hate for her to get lonely when we're not there."

Alia shot Ellis a glance. "Maybe he can stay with her."

"No. He can't. Because he works at the same place I do."

"Oh." The child's face fell.

"But we'll talk about maybe getting a pet." Something that didn't take as much work as a dog did sound pretty appealing. And Lyric missed her parents' dog, too; they'd gotten her not long after she started medical school.

She said goodbye to the teacher, who threw her an apologetic glance, probably because of what Alia had drawn, but it wasn't the woman's fault. She was pretty sure they hadn't coached the kids on what to draw. On impulse, she asked, "Do you know if there's an animal shelter around here?"

"Yes, there's one about a mile from here on Route Fifty-five."

Maybe she would go after Ellis dropped them back off at the hospital.

"I know where it is." The words came from the man beside her. Oh, God, had he thought she'd been hinting that he drive them there?

"Oh, I wasn't implying that you should—"

"I know you weren't. But it's close. If you're really thinking about getting a pet, that is."

She was. At least now. It would be something for Alia to love. A tiny companion who could help the child as much as the child could help a lost or abandoned animal.

She was pretty sure her sister would have approved.

Tessa, this should be you. Why? Why?

But, of course, there was no answer.

Suddenly she was sure of her decision. Maybe Lyric needed something to help her with her grief as well. Some little helper who'd replace sadness with at least a little joy.

"I wasn't thinking about it, but it might be the perfect thing for her. But what about your car?"

"It'll be fine."

Alia put her hand back in Ellis's. "Are you getting a kitten, too?"

"No, but I'll come with you to see what they're like, if that's okay." He looked a little uncomfortable, but he wasn't shaking off her niece's grip. The warmth that had gone through her belly at the park seeped into her again, making her nervous. As did seeing Alia holding his hand. What if she got attached to the man?

Wasn't that another one of her reasons for leaving Vegas? Even though she'd broken it off with Jim before deciding to raise Alia, she'd been half worried that he wouldn't give up and might try to win her back if she stayed. She was pretty sure she would have said no, but why chance it? Part of the reason she'd stayed with him for as long as she had was out of a sense of loneliness. But she'd come to realize he hadn't filled it in any real sense, and she'd finally accepted that he never would.

Neither would Ellis.

So she'd make damn sure he wasn't around Alia enough to break her heart. She was sure he wasn't any more anxious to be a fixture in their lives than she was to have him there. There was nothing to worry about. As soon as they got done at the animal shelter he would be back out of their lives. Or out of Alia's, anyway. And that's all that mattered.

The visitation room at the shelter was busy, surprisingly enough. And the child had not let go of his hand, except for on the drive over there. This wasn't quite what he'd signed up for, but it wasn't like he could just shake her off.

And he was the one who'd offered to drive them over here in the first place. But Lyric had looked stricken when she'd looked at that picture her niece had drawn. He glanced at her now as she peered through the cattery window, where felines of all shapes and sizes were tucked away in different corners or perched on a huge cat tree.

"Are you sure this is what you want to do?" he murmured in a low voice so that Alia couldn't hear. "An animal is a long-term commitment."

"I know. And I actually think it is. But if we find one, I can come back in my own car and pick him or her up."

"Why?"

Her mouth twisted. "Well, you've gone from coming with me to the preschool to volunteering to take us to the animal shelter. I know you said you would, but I don't like asking you to transport him or her, if we find one we agree on."

We agree on.

He knew she was talking about Alia, but the words sent a dart through his midsection. Hell, he'd done this to himself, but at the time it had seemed the right thing to do. And it wasn't like he could back out of it now.

Nor did he want to. Not really. He liked Alia's hand in his more than he wanted to admit, which was part of what made him so uncomfortable. Maybe because he'd once been this child. Or at least had a similar story.

Alia placed her hand on the glass window, and a big scruffy tabby—a slight hitch in his step—moved closer. He seemed to size up the child through the barrier, and then in a surprising move pressed his cheek against the clear surface and rubbed against it.

"Auntie Lyrie! He likes me. Can we have this one?"

Lyric's eyes widened before meeting his. "I don't know, honey. I thought you wanted a kitten."

"He *is* a kitten. And he loves me. He really, really does." The grizzled cat chose that moment to repeat the gesture, and Ellis could almost swear he could hear the animal's purr through the glass.

Lyric knelt and stared at the animal through the glass. "I'm not sure…"

The cat head-butted the glass again, sliding the side of his face over the area where Alia's hand was again. "Please, Auntie Lyrie. He'll cry if we leave him here."

Subtle blackmail? Surely the child wasn't old enough to use tools like that. But Lyric had mentioned that Alia cried when she left her at day care.

Could an animal feel abandonment, like a human?

"Well, let me ask and see what he's like."

She went over to the desk, leaving Ellis alone with the girl. "*You* like him, don't you?" she asked.

He evaded the question as much as he could. "He seems to like you, that's for sure."

"No, he doesn't. He *loves* me."

Damn if the cat didn't sit in front of them as if waiting for Lyric to come back with her verdict. There was an obvious problem with one of his back legs, and as he looked closer, it seemed that his tail had a slight crook to it. Had he been injured?

Looks like that's two strikes against you, bud.

The cat looked up—as if he understood exactly the odds he was up against—with a suddenness that startled Ellis. And yet, he'd still tried to make a connection. A lump formed in his throat—a rare surge of emotion that he hadn't felt since...

Hell. If Lyric didn't take the cat home, he might just have to do it himself. He'd never really thought of having a pet, preferring his independent life, but this wasn't really about him needing companionship so much as it was about the cat needing someone to take care of him. When you had fifty cats in one space it was hard to give them all an opportunity to be adopted, especially one that looked a little rough around the edges.

He'd noticed the more desirable cats had index cards on the window identifying who they were. As his eyes wandered across the groupings, he didn't see anything on this particular cat.

Lyric came over with the attendant, and he found himself almost hoping she would say she didn't want the cat. She sighed and glanced at him. "He's older. And he probably won't want to play with you very much, Alia. Why don't we look at some of the kittens?"

The child glanced up and fixed her aunt with a look that was far beyond her years as the cat limped a few steps away from them as if knowing he was about to be rejected and was distancing himself first. Ellis shouldn't know how the cat felt, but he wondered if he hadn't done some of the same things, because of his mother's disappearance. It's what reactive-attachment disorder meant, right? That if he didn't attach to others, he couldn't be hurt.

"He's hurt. He needs us."

Ellis knelt down. "What if I said I would take this cat home and help him, and you could help another kitty. One that needs someone like you to play with."

"Ellis…" His name came from the woman standing above him. "You don't have to."

"I actually want to. Unless Alia has her heart set on him. Does he have a story?"

The attendant said, "Well…this is Max's second time at the shelter. He was adopted once—a few months ago—and…" She glanced at Lyric as if asking for something.

"Alia, why don't you come with me to look at the kittens while Ellis talks to this nice lady about Max."

"You promise you'll help him? And that I can see him?"

"I do."

The child let go of his hand and went with her aunt to another cattery, where younger cats were.

The attendant handed Ellis an index card that looked like the others that were stuck to the glass. He soon saw why it was not on display. By the time he finished reading it, the knuckles of one hand had curled in on itself in anger and disgust. The decision was made. "I'll take him."

"You can go into a visitation room with him if you want. Even though Max has been through the wringer, he has stayed just as sweet as ever. We all love him here and..." She sized him up. "We want to make sure this never happens to him again."

"It won't. You have my word. Or better yet, you can send someone to check on him from time to time and make sure he's being well treated."

The woman's lip trembled. "Thank you for giving him a chance. He truly deserves it."

In the end, two cat carriers went into his BMW. One with the grizzled old man who'd earned a second shot at happiness and one with a kitten named Shiloh. They were as different as night and day. Shiloh was a multicolored calico who was as spunky and lively as Max was laid-back.

Lyric made sure that Alia was buckled into the car seat and when Ellis went to open the door for her, she stopped him with a hand on his arm. "Thank you. That cat didn't deserve what happened to him, and I was afraid that as much as Alia might have wanted to adopt him, she might hurt him without meaning to. I'll teach her to be careful, but a kitten is a better choice for us." Her hand squeezed for a second and let go. "I guess under that gruff exterior lays a soft heart." She grinned. "I'm talking about Max, of course."

No, she wasn't. But he liked it. And hell if he didn't want to extend that moment of contact between them. He'd better figure out a way to take a few steps back before he wound up with more than a cat. That wouldn't be fair to Alia or her aunt. He did not do emotional attachments, despite Lyric's statement. And if he tried, he had no doubt that he would end up hurting them both. He wasn't sure he could attach to a cat, much less a human being. And from what Lyric had told him about Alia, she, like Max, deserved someone who could love her the way a parent loved a child. This was not some science experiment that you could play with and then toss out and start again. This was Alia's life.

He decided that unless the child asked to come over and visit Max, he wasn't going to offer. It was one thing to be a contact person on a list at a day care and another thing entirely to spend a lot of time with them. So he'd done his good deed for the year and would try not to step up and do anything else.

With his hand on the latch, he gave a pull and opened the door for her without a word, effectively breaking whatever moment there'd been between them. "We need to get the cats home. Do you need me to stop and get anything for yours?"

She glanced at him and then shook her head. "Nope. Alia and I can do it when we pick up my car. There's a big pet store that'll let us bring Shiloh in so she won't have to sit in the car. I'm pretty sure we're going to be in there for a while. Thankfully, my landlord accepts pets."

He hadn't even thought about that, since he owned his place. "I'm glad it worked out for you."

She tilted her head with a frown. "Is something wrong?"

He was acting like a jerk. Well, maybe not a jerk exactly, but he knew he'd gone from friendly to standoffish. But he wasn't sure how to step back any other way. "No. Just didn't expect to wind up adopting a cat."

"Oh, God, I am so—"

"No, I didn't mean it like that. It was my decision and no one else's. And Alia was right, the cat needed someone. And you were right that he needed an adult. At least at this stage, until he's fully healed."

The cat's background had included the fact that a teenager had swung him around by one of his back legs, effectively snapping one of the bones. No vet care had been offered and the bone had healed badly. Fortunately a neighbor had reported a later incident, and the cat had been seized and returned to the shelter. But his tail had been broken so badly that it would be permanently crooked and he was very touchy about having it messed with. He could see why. Ellis would be touchy, too.

In fact, he was, too, just about things other than his physical well-being.

He forced a smile. "It looks like it was fate that we were both there when we were. Max will get a home where he no longer has to worry about being hurt, and Shiloh gets a home where she can run and play to her little heart's content."

"Thanks for offering to let Alia visit him. I promise she won't abuse the privilege."

He was hoping she'd forgotten about that. "It's fine."

It wasn't, but at least she was cognizant of the fact that he wasn't interested in a swinging-door policy.

After closing the car door, he went around to his own side and got in, started the engine and backed out of the shelter's parking lot. And then he headed back the way he'd come just a few hours earlier. When life had been simpler and when he'd had only himself to worry about.

He'd wondered if hiring the behavioral therapist was going to mess up his grant plans.

It had, but not in quite the way he'd thought it would.

If he wasn't careful, this could cost him a lot more than a few pieces of expensive equipment. In fact, if he'd had a heart, he was pretty sure it would be in mortal danger.

So he would just have to make sure that that particular organ had no chance of being resuscitated. By Lyric, her niece or anyone else.

CHAPTER EIGHT

SHILOH BOUNCED OFF the couch and into Alia's arms, much to the child's delight. Despite Lyric's reservations, this had been the right decision after she'd seen the picture her niece had drawn. Hopefully things would continue to go well. A week had passed and Alia was no longer crying when she went to preschool, maybe because she knew that her kitten was at home waiting for her. And her interactions were suddenly a lot more vibrant, according to her teacher. She'd insisted on bringing a picture of Shiloh to class, and Ms. Taylor had taped it to her cubby space, where Alia could see it every time she took something out or put it back.

"We have to go, honey. We'll be late to school."

"Okay." She put Shiloh back down on the couch. "'Bye, Shy. I'll see you after school."

With that she ran toward the door with none of the usual complaints. When Lyric told her mom they'd adopted a cat, she was thrilled and said Lyric's dad was as well. Alia had always loved animals.

What she didn't tell her mom was that she had gone to the shelter with Ellis, since her mom would immediately start formulating various scenarios that would wind up with Lyric married in them. She'd done the same thing when she was dating Jim and, unfortunately, Lyric had gotten caught up in some of those fictional worlds and started to actually believe in fairy tales. Well, no more. She was a little older and a whole lot wiser. At least she hoped she was.

Once she dropped off Alia at school, she headed to work. She hadn't seen Ellis in a couple of days, but that wasn't surprising, since his mornings tended to be a whole lot busier than hers were. At least at first. Lyric was rapidly catching up to him in that area as more and more people heard of the new behavioral endocrinologist's presence at the hospital. He'd warned her that she would have to manage her time in order to not be overrun with patients and doctors needing opinions.

And she had met with the hospital's psychiatrist—with Dr. Lawson's approval—and found her to be very friendly and knowledgeable. Whatever reservations she'd sensed from Ellis hadn't been mirrored in the administrator's position. Maybe it was a territorial issue. Except, contrary to what she might have thought when she'd first met him, he really didn't seem to be.

Oh, well. It didn't matter. What did matter was that Theresa Radner and the behavioral department were behind Lyric's efforts to start a mentoring program that was coordinated by some of the local rehab centers. So far she'd called the one in Merit, the district she and Ellis had visited. And if he didn't have time to go with her to the rest of the areas, Dr. Radner had offered to help her check them out. A bonus was the psychiatrist knew several of the directors of the rehab centers and could act as a liaison between New Mercy and the centers.

She breezed into the hospital, her mood light for once, anxious to get her day started. She exited the elevator onto the fourth floor and headed to her office, only to find Ellis outside of it waiting for her.

"Am I late for something?" She glanced at her phone. She'd been extraordinarily careful to be on time ever since their first bristly meeting.

"No, just wanted to catch you before your day started."

"It looks like yours already has."

He shook his head. "I'm just an early bird, although my new roommate has been keeping me up late at nights."

Shock made her go very still. His new roommate?

As if sensing her surprise, his eyebrows went up. "Max? The cat? Surely you haven't forgotten our trip to the shelter."

Before she could stop it, every muscle in

her body seemed to relax at once, threatening to send her slithering to the ground. She quickly stiffened her back. "Of course. I thought maybe you'd rented out a room or something."

The or-something part was really where her head had been parked. Although to find a special someone a week after they'd kissed? That would have changed her view of him, although she wasn't sure why. The kiss had meant nothing. To either of them.

Right?

Right. She'd learned her lesson when it came to that. She wasn't going to let herself get caught up in those kinds of mind games ever again. Nor was she going to let her mom blow things out of proportion, which is why she'd kept things such a secret.

"No, I think two curmudgeons are enough for one bachelor pad."

"I think you're probably right. Especially two perpetual bachelors. Although *curmudgeon* is a pretty apt term as well."

"You've been talking to Dave."

Oh, great. She really didn't want him to think she and the Realtor had been gossiping about him. She had only talked to Dave one other time since signing the lease on her place. He'd called to see how things were going and to let her know if she ever needed someone to talk to, to feel free to contact him. She didn't need someone, so she'd never called him back. She'd halfway wondered if he'd been hinting at wanting to go out on a date with her, but if so, she wasn't interested. He was a nice guy, but he certainly wasn't…

That was one blank she was not going to fill in.

"Not much, no." She didn't remember Dave actually using the word *perpetual*, just the fact he'd made a point of saying Ellis was never going to marry. And her earlier attempt at humor had evidently missed the mark.

"Hmm."

She unlocked her office door and motioned him in. "How is Max, anyway?"

"He's actually at the vet's office this morning—the real reason I'm here so early. He has to have the piece of his tail below the break amputated because of nerve damage and the fear that he might injure it more or get it caught somewhere."

"Oh, no! Poor guy. How's his leg?"

"He'll always have a limp—the vet says it's due to a joint fusing near where his break was. He assured me it looks more painful than it actually is, and he gets around fine. It makes him look tough."

Like his owner, although Ellis definitely didn't have a limp.

"A shorter tail will make him look even tougher." She sat behind her desk and waited for him to find a seat, as well. "So what did you want to talk to me about?"

"I wanted to run something by you. The grant donor is having a small ceremony at his office building to officially present the hospital with a check. Jack would like each person who will benefit from it to explain their vision and how they hope it will help the people in our city."

"But, I'm not sure how that affects..." Her

brain stopped for a second before restarting. "You mean the addiction-mentor program is actually getting some of the money?"

"Yes. Jack wanted it, and seeing that girl on the ground convinced me we need to help if we can."

"Alisha."

"What?"

"That's her name." She wasn't sure why it was so important that he recognize that there was a name that went with the face, but it was.

"Okay. Seeing *Alisha* convinced me."

"Sorry. I didn't mean that to come out the way it did." She paused to think through what he'd said. "What do I need to do exactly? Write up a revised proposal so Jack can read it at the ceremony?"

"No, he'd like us—as in you and me—to both be there and give a presentation."

"Can't you just roll mine into yours?" The thought of having to speak and possibly ruin the hospital's chances of getting the grant horrified her. "What if they change their minds after hearing me?"

"Not a chance. Just talk to them the way you presented it to me. You'll do great." He looked at her. "And I'll be right there, Lyric, I promise."

The way he'd said it made goose bumps roll up her arms. Like it included more than just the presentation. But she'd better disabuse herself of that idea and fast.

"Jack really wants me to do this?"

"Yes. And so do I."

He did? Lord. First they'd revived a girl, then he'd agreed to be Alia's emergency pickup and then they'd adopted cats together. And now they were going to be giving a presentation? Together? A warning light went off in her head.

I hear those wheels turning, Ly. Do not take his words to mean more than they're meant to.

A thought hit her. "When is it? I have Alia. If it's at night…"

"It is. Tell you what, she can come with us.

You can watch her during my speech, and I can watch her during yours."

"I couldn't ask that. Maybe my mom can come. How far out is the date?"

He smiled. "It's this coming Monday."

Today was Wednesday. There was no way her mom could get here by then. "What would you do if I had six children and had no one to watch them?"

"But you don't." He leaned forward. "Do you want this as much as I do?"

Another shiver went down her spine. Bigger, this time. Were they still talking about the money? She swallowed. "I do. Very much so."

"Good."

She tried to shake her thoughts free. "What is the dress code?"

"Suit and tie for men, a suit or dress for women." He smiled. "I'll be honest. I don't think anyone has ever come in and wowed Jack so quickly or completely."

Did he think she'd manipulated him? "I—I

just feel strongly about it. I wasn't trying to—"

"I know. And I wasn't implying you were. I was just surprised. And yet maybe not as surprised now as I was that first day."

She had no idea what he meant and was too afraid to pick apart what he'd said, just in case she took a wrong turn and misunderstood something. "Are you sure you can't just tack my presentation onto yours?"

"I believe in giving credit where credit is due. I think you're going to be a wonderful asset to this hospital. And people in the community need to hear your passion, the way Jack did. The way I did."

He'd never said anything like that to her before and it was hard not to feel swept off her feet by it. But if she was smart, she'd keep those feet firmly planted on the ground. Where they belonged.

"Okay, I'll try. But I can't guarantee not to fall flat on my face."

"You won't. I'm sure of it."

"How about if I write up the presentation

and send it to you for your thoughts? I'm sure you've done these before. I haven't." She couldn't help but think New Mercy was right where she belonged, despite her first missteps and uncertainties about being here.

"I have. I'm sure you'll do fine, but I'll be happy to look at it, if it will make you feel better."

"It definitely will, thank you. If I get it to you by Friday, will that be enough time?" She couldn't believe she was just now hearing about this. Surely it had been in the works for a while. Unless she'd just been added to the recipient list. Maybe Ellis wasn't kidding, and he'd had to be convinced before he was willing to let a cent of that grant money leave his hands. Should she be irritated…or grateful?

The latter.

Lyric's phone buzzed and she glanced at the readout. "It's the ER, wonder what they want…" She picked it up and answered. "Dr. Westphal here."

The words on the other line ran together

for a second or two until one name suddenly stood out and made her blood turn to ice.

Alisha.

The patient they had just been talking about was down in the ER and her sister was asking for them.

"What happened?"

The words *coded* and *life support* stood out among the others, all given in a crisp, matter-of-fact voice by whoever was on the other end. Her heart pounded until she thought it was going to explode. She realized the staff member was still talking and that she was just sitting there frozen. Ellis took the phone from her nerveless fingers and talked to whoever was speaking. Unlike her, he asked lots of questions and listened to the responses before hanging up.

"Come on, Lyric. Alisha's sister is asking for us. Her parents are there, as well."

Somehow she got up from her desk, feeling totally numb. This couldn't be happening. She had done CPR. Ellis had administered naloxone, and they'd gotten her back. And now, a little over a week later, she was back in the hospital. But this time, she hadn't regained consciousness.

She followed Ellis to the elevator and down they went to the first floor, all thoughts of the grant and presentation wiped away. He'd explained that Alisha had hidden a small packet of heroin in her room and had tried to inject herself with a smaller dose this time, but the thought was that the drugs had been laced with fentanyl, making even that small dose more potent than her slight frame could handle. Only this time, everything had happened in private, away from the eyes and ears of people who might have helped. A late dose of naloxone had helped revive her, but her brain had been without oxygen for too long. Tests were still being done, but they suspected she could be brain-dead.

The doors opened, and Lyric stepped out of the elevator, the contents of her stomach swirling. She'd just insisted on Ellis using the girl's name, and now it seemed so ludicrous. What did that matter in the grand scheme of things? A girl was dead or possibly dying and no one had been there to help. There'd been no mentor program…no safety net to help catch a girl who'd been free-falling toward oblivion.

An ache settled in Lyric's chest that she doubted would ever go away.

She felt numb. She hugged the grieving parents, listening as they thanked her for trying to save their daughter the last time. Listened as they wished there had been some kind of help for Alisha. Listened as the words *organ donation* were mentioned in hushed tones.

She wanted to yell at them to stop. To say that maybe things would be okay, but deep down she knew they weren't going to be. Not this time. Finally she turned as someone tapped her. Alisha's sister fell into her arms with gasping sobs, a world of grief and guilt in the tears. A guilt Lyric could relate to all too well. Because she'd felt the exact same guilt after her own sister had died.

She'd tried for years to find Tessa some help—she and her parents both had—but every ounce of success had been met with a pound of failure. She and her parents had sacrificed so much in terms of time and money... and love. If only Lyric had been able to...

Suddenly she knew she was going to give that presentation to make sure neither Tessa nor Alisha were forgotten. Not by her. Not by Ellis. Not by this hospital.

"Are you okay?" Ellis slid a cup of hospital coffee into Lyric's hands, her fingers icy against his.

He was worried. He knew she'd taken Alisha's drug overdose seriously, but seeing the color drain from her face as she'd held her phone to her ear had made him realize something terrible had happened. Doctors were supposed to be objective parties, able to separate themselves from what went on with their patients. He was the master at doing that. But they all had that one patient who touched them in a way that others couldn't. There was no rhyme or reason, and this was evidently

Lyric's "someone." And he was pretty sure it was because of her sister.

"No. I'm really not. God, how could this have happened? She wasn't a habitual user. She was experimenting."

"Sometimes that's all it takes."

They sat on the sofa in his office. He'd pushed back his first surgery by an hour, unable to leave Lyric like this.

"But she seemed to be interested in getting help. Her sister is still in a program, in fact."

"I know." He took a swig of his own coffee, trying to think of something to say that would help.

Lyric kicked off her shoes and curled into the corner of the couch, seeming very small and unsure. "I'm wracking my brain for a way we could have done things differently."

Her beautiful eyes were clouded with the sadness that came with their profession. It was the unfortunate reality of working in health care, but something inside of him wanted to find a way to wipe away her pain. But there was no pat answer. No magic formula. All he could do was speak the truth and hope it helped.

"We had very little time with either of those girls. The fact that Alisha's sister even remembered your name is shocking."

Although Lyric probably would have taken it even harder if they'd gotten the news secondhand. And with organ donations the way they were, there was no doubt they would have heard about Alisha eventually.

Right now they were waiting on the verdict of the latest EEG and CAT scan of her head, although things really didn't look good.

As if the universe had heard his thoughts, his phone buzzed at almost the exact same time as hers did.

She sat up, her back going ramrod-straight. "Here it comes."

Ellis looked down at the text, which had the results of both tests. They confirmed what the specialists thought. There was no brain function. The only thing keeping her alive were the machines.

Alisha would never regain consciousness.

Would never hug her parents or graduate from high school.

"I'm sorry, Lyric. I wish it was better news."

"So do I. It's so hard to believe." She paused for a second before continuing. "Do they do anything to honor the donors?"

"Do anything?" He wasn't sure what she meant. "Like a memorial service?"

"No, like a walk where we can stand in the aisles to acknowledge the decision to save others' lives through organ donation."

New Mercy had been doing that for almost a year. It was always a solemn procession with family and hospital staff alike participating. "We do. A text will be sent out with the time. As many staff participate as possible. I have a couple of patients waiting on organs. It's a strange mixture of sadness and celebration because she'll be helping others, even if we couldn't help her. But we tried, Lyric. Know that. We genuinely tried."

He wasn't sure why it was so important for her to know that, but something urged him to back up the words with a physical touch. So he slid his arm around her, feeling her scoot closer as she laid her head against his shoulder. She gave a slight sigh, which burrowed into his chest and did a number on something in there. Something that made him want to stay right there and not move. At least for a while. And that was not like him. At all.

"I'm not normally this weepy, I promise," she said. "Today was just hard."

Maybe he wasn't the only one struggling through unfamiliar territory.

"I know. But as hard as it is, Alisha will do some good beyond just organ donation. Because of her, others may have access to better services than she did. And maybe this will be the wakeup call her sister needs to get her life straight. Maybe one day, she'll be one of those mentors who helps others like her sister."

"I hope so."

His arm was still around her, but the weight of her body felt good against him. Maybe he was drawing some comfort from her, as well. Kind of like Max, the cat?

Ha! That cat had no problems forming attachments. Ellis knew he should move away, but it couldn't hurt to stay here a little longer. "Done with your coffee?"

"Yes, thanks." She handed it to him, shifting slightly as he set the cup on the glass-topped coffee table in front of him. Something about this whole thing seemed strangely…comfortable, in a way he'd not felt with other women.

He chalked it up to supporting someone he'd had a shared experience with. And not that kiss. The shared experience of losing a patient.

He'd soon forget any of this ever happened. Right?

Except no matter how many times he recited that mantra, another little voice was whispering in the background that it was all one big lie. And that if he didn't move away soon, something irrevocable was going to happen.

So he patted her shoulder. "I probably need to see about my surgical patient, but feel free to stay here as long as you want."

She sat up in a hurry, making him regret

saying anything. "No, I'm fine, and I need to check on some things as well. Jacob Sellers is coming in with his parents in the morning so they can administer the first actual dose of his growth hormone, so I need to make sure I'm ready for that. And I want to work on my presentation."

"You don't have to do that right now."

"I want to. While everything is still fresh in my mind."

While what was still fresh? Certainly not this exact moment of finding themselves snuggled together on the couch like an old married couple.

No. Not a married couple. Or a couple of any kind. Despite his wandering imagination.

He stood, trying to convince himself that he hadn't done anything wrong, had merely comforted a coworker the way he would comfort anyone. Except he'd never felt the need to comfort anyone before. In fact, he normally left the scene at the first hint of tears of any kind, whether it was in his personal or professional life.

And yet, Lyric was no longer crying. And she seemed ready to get back to work, so maybe he'd done the right thing after all.

At least he hoped so. Otherwise he was going to have a mess on his hands that wouldn't be as easy to clean up as it had been to make.

CHAPTER NINE

ON THURSDAY, SHE'D just typed the final lines of her presentation when news came that Alisha York's organs were viable and would be harvested. Her lungs, liver and one of her kidneys would go to recipients in this hospital, while her heart and other tissue would be transported to other facilities. Lyric had seen Jacob Sellers this morning and had helped his parents administer the first of many shots. They'd done great, the hope of a new start to their son's life a stark contrast to what Alisha's parents and sister were now going through.

Ellis had been so kind yesterday—there hadn't been a hint of impatience at her emotionalism. It was a relief, really. He could have given her a lecture on getting too involved. But he hadn't. Instead, he'd wrapped his arm around her and murmured comforting words to her. She couldn't remember everything he'd said, but she'd felt cared for in a way that she hadn't felt in a very long time.

She had no idea where the tears had come from. She couldn't remember the last time she'd cried over a patient. But Ellis had seemed to understand.

At least until the end, when he'd suddenly seemed uncomfortable.

Had she given off some kind of weird, needy vibes at some point? Lord, she hoped not. That was the last thing she needed.

But she was working on it. She'd almost convinced herself that what had happened in his office was an anomaly. Something that wouldn't be repeated, if she could help it.

That's all she could do, since she couldn't go back and erase the feeling of his arm around her. Nor did she want to. But that didn't mean he had to know that.

She emailed a copy of the presentation to Ellis. She'd told him she'd have it to him by Friday, but the words had poured out of her once she started writing, so she decided to go with it. She glanced at her phone just as it pinged. Staff had been invited to join in what the hospital called an Honor Walk that would start in an hour. Lyric had a short internal debate about whether she should go or not, before deciding she needed to. She not only wanted to honor Alisha's life, but also wanted to support the family in these moments of grief, even if they never knew she was there.

Should she text Ellis?

No. He would have received the same message. Whether he went or not was up to him. She was pretty sure she wouldn't turn into a waterworks on him this time. She'd pretty much cried herself out yesterday. One thing she could be glad of was that the girl's struggle was over. She wouldn't linger in some institution—hooked to machines—with no one quite sure as to what to do with her.

She finished up some loose ends on some paperwork and then went down to ICU, where other staff members were already lining up. She spotted Ellis about ten yards up the line and gave him a quick wave. He made no move to come over to where she was, so she stayed in place. Five minutes later, the doors at the end of the hallways swung open and Alisha's bed came into sight.

She swallowed as the transplant team slowly pushed the hospital bed, various cords and tubes strung over the back and snaking up poles that were attached to the bed. Behind Alisha came her parents, her sister and several people she didn't recognize but seemed to be members of the girl's family.

Staff had been through this before, but it was still a terrible and yet awesome sight to see so many people as they said goodbye to one life and placed the patient in the hands of the skilled surgeons who would have a massive undertaking to get everything completed in a timely manner.

Alisha passed by where she was standing, and Lyric had to resist the urge to touch the child's hand. Glancing over at Ellis, she caught him looking at her. Maybe wondering if she was going to lose it again? She wasn't. If anything, she felt kind of numb. She'd been honest. What had happened yesterday was a rarity. Maybe because there was no one she trusted enough with those kinds of emotions.

Not anymore.

Except she had yesterday. Did that mean she trusted Ellis? She wasn't sure. But she sensed he wasn't really the ideal person to let down her guard around. Maybe because of how controlled he seemed most of the time.

Alisha's sister walked by, sobbing softly by her mother's side. She saw Lyric and hesitated. Lyric mouthed "it's okay." And that seemed to help the girl, whose dragging feet seemed to pick up the pace. This would probably be the last time she saw this family. At least she hoped so. Not because she didn't want to see them, but because she didn't want to meet under these circumstances again. If her program proved successful, Lyric hoped the emergency room would see a reduction in patients like Alisha, and those who were physically and emotionally addicted to drugs.

At least, that was her dream. What she hoped this grant money would help with.

As the procession rounded the corner and was gone from sight, staff members slowly disbursed and went back to work. She was turning to do the same when Ellis caught up with her. "Hey, I got your email. I haven't had a chance to read your presentation yet, but I will tonight, if Max lets me." He gave a quick smile.

"No hurry. I just finished it sooner than I thought I would and decided to send it on over."

"I haven't even started mine yet, so you're ahead of me."

She stopped and propped her back against the wall behind her as a thought hit her. "Will any of your patients get Alisha's organs?"

"Yes. One. The transplant team will be doing the surgery. In fact, the patient has already been prepped and they're just waiting for the signal to head to the operating room."

"I'm glad. Not about Alisha, but that she'll

be able to help some other people. I'd like to think she'd be glad, too."

"I think she would. Her parents are doing a good thing." He glanced down at her, green eyes sliding over her face.

"Yes, they are."

He paused. "Did Jacob Sellers come in?"

"Yes, I'm sorry, I thought I told you he was due in today."

"You did. I just had a full surgical schedule today, so couldn't stop in. I take it he did well?"

She nodded. "He did great. So did Mom and Dad. They're not going to have any problems administering the meds."

"Good to hear."

She swallowed, feeling tongue-tied all of a sudden. Maybe because they hadn't talked about what had happened in his office yesterday. Well, they had a little, but they hadn't resolved where they stood with each other.

As far as she was concerned, they were coworkers with cases that just so happened to overlap. Laying her head on his shoulder wasn't what she should be doing with him. The sooner she remembered that, the better.

"Max still doing okay?"

"He is. Shiloh and Alia?"

"Thick as thieves and doing great. Once we get our own permanent place, we may even add another kitten so Shiloh isn't alone during the day when Alia starts kindergarten in the fall."

"I didn't realize she was almost five."

"Yes, her birthday is next month, as hard as that is to believe." Also hard to believe was the fact that her sister would be gone for seven months by then. Would Alisha's family feel the same way once that period of time passed?

Undoubtedly.

"Will your parents come out to celebrate?"

"Yes. They're excited. So is Alia."

He seemed to hesitate for a second. "Can I ask you to take a look at something?"

"Of course. Is it about a patient?"

She gave an internal eye roll. What else would he be asking her to look at?

"Not exactly."

Intrigued, she gave a nod. If it wasn't a patient, then what?

"Where is it?"

"At my house."

That made her blink. "Okay. When?"

"This afternoon, if you have time. If not it can wait until later."

"I should be able to. I'll have to pick Alia up at two so I'll have her with me if you need it to be later than that."

"Do you have any more patients today?"

She shook her head. "No, just some paperwork, but I can do it tomorrow, if need be."

Ellis was breathtaking today in black jeans and a white button-down shirt. His sleeves were rolled up, revealing tanned forearms, the muscles in them well defined. She had to harden herself to keep from staring.

"Can you follow me over?"

"Sure."

He gave her the address in case they got separated and said it was about a fifteen-minute drive from the hospital. Her curiosity was killing her. What on earth could he want her to look at? Unless it was some question on carpet color or something. If so, he was going to be horribly disappointed because she was not good at decorating. She'd always kept to whites and used throw pillows to give a punch of color. They were easy to exchange, if she wanted to, although she'd had the same set for the last five years. She and Tessa had gone shopping for her sofa and ottoman together, in fact. The pieces were getting a little worn after all this time but she couldn't bear to get rid of them. It was one of the last things the sisters had done together before Tessa's addiction had gotten really bad.

True to his word, they were at his place in no time, parking in front of his house. Like his BMW, his house was nice, but not over-the-top. The landscaping looked professionally cared for, which she could understand, since he worked so much.

She turned off the car, got out and met him at the front door. There, he said, "Feel free to say no. I won't be offended."

Lyric gulped, her mind swirling in a hundred different directions, but none of it made any sense. She was pretty sure he hadn't brought her here to have sex with her. And why would he assume she might say no to whatever it was. "Okay."

This time the word wasn't quite as sure as it had been earlier. If he did ask her something unexpected, would she turn him down?

Of course she would, one side of her brain said with a pointed look. Except the other side was a little less sure of itself and a little more eager to find out what this mysterious "something" was.

He opened the door, and waited for her to slide past him. Once inside, she glanced around. A leather sectional took up most of the space, looking long and comfortable enough to...

To nothing, Ly. No thinking along those lines.

Hadn't she just said she shouldn't trust this man with her emotions?

"It's in my shop."

His shop as in store? She glanced around, but saw no sign of anything like that, unless it was in a different part of the house. "Where is that?"

"Out back."

A meow came from behind her, making her turn.

Max!

He was slowly making his way toward them, the limp from his hind leg still evident. And his tail was definitely shorter. By about three inches. She knelt in front of him. "Hi, bud. How're you doing?"

He rubbed his cheek against her hand and kept moving, until he made a complete circle around her and came back to where he started. "He looks like he's healing up well."

"He's doing great, although I will say that he's a bed hog."

She laughed, although the thought of this cat snuggling against Ellis's lanky form made her stomach tense in a way she didn't like. Before she could stop the words, she said, "He's a lucky boy."

He looked at her for a long minute. "I'd say we both are."

Leading the way into the kitchen, he stopped in front of the refrigerator, Max still on their heels. "Would you like something to drink?"

"Actually a beer, if you have one."

He glanced at her with raised eyebrows that she thought showed a hint of admiration. "I think I'll join you." Opening the door, he took out two longnecks, cradling them between his index and ring fingers, palm up. The bottles clanked together invitingly.

"I don't keep alcohol at home because of Alia, so this is a treat."

He laughed. "I never thought of beer as a treat, but I can see your point."

He opened the bottles with an opener he had hanging on the side of a cabinet. After handing her one of the bottles, he tipped his head and took a long pull at his, his throat moving in a way that caught her right below the ribs.

Stifling the urge to stare, she quickly followed his lead, letting the bitter brew linger on her tongue for a minute before she let it flow down her throat.

"Mmm, thanks." She leaned a hip against the cabinet and took another sip.

"You're welcome. The shop is just out here." He opened a sliding glass door and, using a foot to block Max from getting out, he stepped out onto a brick patio. The red herringbone fit in with the brick facade of the house's exterior.

"You have a beautiful home."

His head tilted. "Thanks. Max is making me spend more time inside it than I have in the past."

His voice sounded strange. Like he wasn't crazy about that fact. Or was it that he was so busy at the hospital, that he didn't get a chance to be here?

"Alia has done the same for me."

And she realized it was true. Her niece was quickly making her into a homebody, something she'd never seen herself as being, although she'd eventually hoped she'd have a family of her own.

She'd thought that would be with Jim, at one point. And actually, she wasn't sure why she'd ever thought that. Looking back, she could see that his focus was on his job. Most of their time together was spent in bed with very little interaction outside of that.

What had she been thinking?

A large building sat at the back of the yard, looking almost like a barn, except it couldn't be, since they were just on the outskirts of the city of Atlanta. What in the world did he need something this for?

Leading the way back to it, Ellis unlocked a side door and motioned her inside, clicking on a light. She blinked, standing there for a second, unsure at first of what she was looking at. There were several worktables that held various saws and drills, along with machines she didn't recognize. On several of the tables were pieces of wood. Some were spindles and others had curved legs.

That's right. His calluses. He said he'd gotten them from woodworking. She noticed a rocker made out of a light-colored wood sitting off to the side. It was gorgeous, and the large curved back looked like it was made from a single piece of wood. "Wow, Ellis. This is beautiful. You made this?"

"I did. Do you like it?" He moved over and gripped the back of it, pushing it slightly so that it rocked back and forth.

It was gorgeous.

"Like it? I love it. Who did you make this for, or do you sell your pieces?"

"I do sometimes, although I don't really like doing it. Dave has one of my rocking chairs. As does Jack."

The hospital administrator? Well, she'd thought they were friends, so that made sense. "Are their chairs just like this one?"

"Not exactly. I make the backs just a bit different, so that each one is unique."

She studied it. The spindles coming off the arms of the chair were like the ones she saw on another table. "How many of these have you made?"

"This is number six. I put a little stainless tag under the seat of each one listing its number." He shrugged. "I experimented with different pieces of furniture before realizing what I really like to make are rocking chairs."

"I can see why. Is this what you wanted me to look at?"

"Yes."

He wanted her to see it? Why? There was no question it was beautiful, but she was a little confused. It was like he was giving her a small peek at his life, without telling her what he expected her to do with it.

But she liked that he trusted her enough to let her see this. Especially since he'd only made six of these. Had he brought other women here?

Something she didn't need to be thinking about. Especially since she'd pictured herself taking Max's place in bed just a few minutes earlier.

And what had he meant that he wouldn't be offended if she said no? Maybe he wanted her opinion on one of his projects?

"If you want to know what I think, I would say this is a work of art. The new owner will be very lucky."

"And if I wanted Alia to have it?"

"Alia?" She frowned. "I don't understand."

"You said her birthday is next month. And I don't have anyone to give this to."

Shock dried her mouth, making it hard to speak. "Ellis, I can't accept this. Not without paying for it. Unless it costs a fortune…not that it wouldn't be worth it." Her words were tumbling out faster and faster. She was trying very hard not to read too much into his offer, although her heart was racing ahead and saying all kinds of crazy things. "I don't think you should be—"

"I'm not selling it. I want Alia to have it."

Her throat tightened. Surely he had family who would want something he made. "What about your parents? Or siblings?"

"I don't have any."

None? They hadn't talked about his relatives, but surely he had someone. Except he said that he didn't. And the way he said it—

matter-of-fact, as if it was no big deal. But it was. Didn't he know that family was everything? At least to her.

The tightness in her throat grew. "I'm sorry. I didn't know."

"It's okay. My mom's been gone for a long time, and I don't have brothers or sisters."

He didn't offer any more information; evidently his dad wasn't in the picture and his grandparents were no longer alive, either, or he would have mentioned them.

"But there must be someone else you want to have it."

He gave the rocker another slight push. "I really just make these to unwind, so I'm not interested in making money off of them. I just want someone to enjoy it. Someone like Alia. She can rock Shiloh in it."

How would she feel seeing this in her house day in and day out, knowing he'd made it— that he'd wanted Alia to have it? She wasn't sure.

This would be something her niece could pass down to her own children someday. "I don't know, Ellis. And can I just say, you make me feel like a slug. The only thing I do on my off time is clean house and maybe pull a few weeds."

"You are no slug. You work hard. Alia is very fortunate to have you. More than you could ever know."

The words contained a sincerity that shook her to the core.

"Thank you. I appreciate that." She took a deep breath, suddenly knowing what she was going to do, whether it was wise or not. "I know she would love it. It'll go nicely with her bed and dresser. As long as Shiloh doesn't use it as a scratching post."

"The oak is pretty tough. I think it can withstand a scratch or two. And if not, it'll give the piece character."

Character, huh?

She motioned toward the seat. "Can I? I have to admit, I'll probably be sharing this with Alia…and Shiloh."

"Please."

Lowering herself onto the smooth wooden

surface, she was surprised at how well the chair cradled her. The seat was curved in a slight *S* shape that supported her bottom and thighs—the height was perfect, as well. It was comfortable. Very comfortable. And Ellis had carved this out by hand, put it together piece by piece, sanding it, smoothing a protective finish along each curve and hollow.

It was on the tip of her tongue to ask him again if he was sure about giving this away, but she sensed he wouldn't appreciate her throwing back his offer in his face. "It's wonderful. I didn't see one in the house."

"I have one in each of the three bedrooms."

Bedrooms. Including his?

That's right. He said he'd built six of them. If he'd given ones to Jack and Dave, that left four, including this one. So this would only be the third chair he'd given away. A strange warmth went through her, sweeping from her belly up through her chest and into her face. "I'm honored."

"It's nothing. It'll be a relief not to have fifty chairs gathering dust out here."

It might be nothing to him. But it meant a lot to her. "Can you keep it here until her birthday? I'd like to sneak it into her room while she's at school and put a bow on it. I imagine she and Shiloh will get a lot of rocking time in."

"I can. If you let me know when you want it, I can bring it over."

She looked a bit dubious. "In your BMW?"

"I fit the last two in there, so, yes."

"Okay, thank you, then. Her birthday is the fifteenth, so if we could do it in the early afternoon…" She blinked, an idea coming to mind. "Actually, why don't you stay for cake afterward. I'm sure Alia would love it."

"I'll have to see what my schedule looks like that day, but if it's not too hectic, I should be able to."

He didn't sound all that thrilled, and she could have kicked herself. She was doing exactly what she'd warned herself about: making a bigger deal out of this chair than she should have. And what was she thinking inviting him? Hadn't she already lectured herself about not letting Alia get attached to him? It wouldn't take much. After all, look at her, Lyric herself was quickly becoming enamored with the pediatrician. She'd almost swooned over him gifting them a simple chair.

She'd made that same mistake with Jim, and look how that had turned out.

She couldn't exactly withdraw the invitation, though, without having to make up some kind of explanation, so she did the next best thing. "Either way is fine. And if you'd rather I pick up the chair and save you a trip, I can do that."

"It's fine. I can bring it. I just don't want to intrude on family time. I know how important that must be."

Said as if he didn't know. Or maybe he just wanted to emphasize to her that he wasn't part of their family so she didn't get any funny ideas. He needn't worry, if that was the case.

She wasn't interested in making him part of it.

She took another drink of her beer, rocking in the chair. "You wouldn't be intruding." Time to change the subject. "So you've made six chairs. How many more do you have in the works?"

"Two. It's easier to cut out multiple parts at a time, while the machines are set up for them."

Who would he be giving those chairs to? None of her business. She didn't even want to think about another woman squealing at the sight of one of these rockers.

She cleared her throat. "That makes sense."

He leaned a hip on a workbench and watched her, his own beer making a trip or two to his lips and hanging there. Her mouth watered. The man was incredible, like a ginger Adonis, there was no denying that.

"So what was Vegas like?"

The question took her by surprise, although it shouldn't have. She'd had several people at the hospital ask the same.

"Vegas is kind of hard to describe. It's glitzy like what you see in advertisements, but there are also parts of it that are kind of rough."

"Kind of like Atlanta."

"Hmm…maybe, but in a different kind of way. It can be a great place to live. But it can also be hard when the reality of day-to-day life doesn't match up with the wealthy image."

One side of his mouth hiked a bit. "I could say the same about this city. I'm sure they both have their own sets of challenges, maybe just in different areas."

"Challenges. That's a great way to put it." She leaned her head against the back of the chair. "I can't believe how comfortable this is. I'll have to be careful or I could fall asleep."

She took the last drink of her beer, then let him take the bottle and toss it along with his into a nearby recycling can.

"Not such a bad problem, is it?"

"It is when I still have to go pick up Alia later and get her some dinner."

He tucked his hands into his back pockets. "I'd better let you go then."

Except, Lyric didn't want to go. She wanted to stay here and learn more about him, while rocking in his luscious chair. She couldn't remember a time she'd felt so relaxed.

Had to be the beer.

Or the company.

No, definitely the beer.

She got up, her fingers lingering on the arm of the chair, then trailing across it as if loath to leave it here. And really, it was true.

"I'm really glad you like it."

"I love it." The words came from a place in her heart that she hadn't opened in a while. And with it came the slightest trickle of fear. What was she doing here? Was she falling for him? Or was it just about the chair?

Right now, she didn't know and she didn't care. All she knew was it seemed like he'd given her a glimpse into what made Ellis... Ellis. He'd trusted her with that, was willing to share a piece of it with her in the form of this chair. And she wasn't sure what to do with it.

They were about five feet from each other, and Lyric couldn't stop looking at him. Was suddenly remembering the shivery sensation of being in his arms with his mouth on hers. The impossible cascade of feelings that had come along with his touch. And the memory of that was...impossible to forget.

Not good. Not smart. But there it was.

"Lyric?"

His voice was low. Soft. A husky timbre she recognized from the images that were currently dancing in her head. And the look in his eyes...

Mesmerizing.

"Yes?" She barely squeezed the word out from between suddenly dry lips.

He was going to kiss her again.

And she was going to let him.

"How soon do you have to pick up Alia?"

"Not for almost an hour." Her breathing grew heavy as his question drew up all kinds of dangerous possibilities. None of them chaste. None of them platonic. But all of them hoping he was thinking what she was thinking.

One side of his mouth kicked up. "Sixty whole minutes."

She decided to tease him just a bit, although she still wasn't sure what he was getting at. "Time enough to build another chair?"

His chuckle was low and earthy. "Not quite what I had in mind. But watching you touch that chair..." His gaze skated over her. "Come here, Lyric."

Oh, yes. He was definitely thinking what she'd hoped he was thinking. There was no way he wasn't.

"Do I have dirt on my face?" She took a step or two closer, then his fingers were at her wrist hauling her against him.

"No. No dirt. Not even a speck."

Tilting her head to look back at him, she finally allowed herself to smile, her heart feeling lighter than it had in weeks. "Well since we only have an hour, Ellis, let's not spend it in idle chitchat."

"Idle? No, what I have in mind is anything but idle."

With that, he lowered his head and slid his lips over hers.

CHAPTER TEN

HE HADN'T BROUGHT her here to kiss her, but now that he was, he saw the folly in even thinking he'd be able to bring her here and *not* kiss her.

But for some reason, he'd needed her to see that chair. And in seeing her fingers slide across the warm wood… Well, it had brought all kinds of X-rated images alive in his head. He wanted those hands on him, doing the same things to his body. He wanted it all, to hell with the consequences. They were both adults. They could handle it.

And it wasn't like he was asking her for forever or anything.

That last thought created a little glimmer of doubt—doubt that was quickly erased by the sound she made in her throat when he deepened the kiss.

Ah, that sound. Luscious and heady. Just like the woman herself.

His teeth skimmed across her lower lip. She tasted of beer and mysterious things. Things he wanted to explore in depth. And he wanted to do it here in this room, where he spent most of his off time.

He'd been honest when he said he didn't spend a whole lot of time in the house, although Max was changing that out of necessity. And he'd never invited a woman to see his workshop before, had never felt the need. He'd done all he needed to do with them in his bedroom and then had sent them on their way the next day.

So why Lyric? And why here?

Not something he wanted to thinking about right now.

His hands smoothed up her back, the silky beige blouse sliding up, leaving warm, bare skin that his palm couldn't resist.

His other hand went to the back of her head, tipping it a bit more so that his lips could find her jawline and trail down the side of her neck, relishing every inch along the way.

Lyric moaned, and like her name, it was pure music.

"I want you," he groaned against her ear. "Here. Now."

Her answer was to bring his mouth back to hers, her kisses deep and wet and capable of stealing things he might not be able to get back.

Right now, he didn't care.

His arm curved around the small of her back, pressing her tight against him. He hoped to ease the ache that was growing harder to ignore.

But, hell, he didn't want to just throw her down and rush to the finish line. He had an hour. He wanted to use it. Every second of it. If he was going to regret this later on, he was going to make sure he had plenty of reasons to do so.

He walked her slowly backward toward the door, the only safe flat surface he could think of out here other than the bare concrete floor. And when he arrived at his destination, that ache he'd been trying to ignore became a drum that beat against him.

He couldn't remember his need being this damn strong. This damn impossible to control.

He gathered her hands in one of his and slowly raised them above her head. If she touched him right now, that control would be lost in an instant. And he wanted a whole lot more than an instant. He wanted the hour. Every single minute of it.

Looking into brown eyes that had gone completely dark, he leaned over and kissed the side of her nose, her mouth, the tip of her chin, before settling back on her mouth. This time, she arched toward him with a fierceness that made him harden beyond belief. He let her hands go so that he could haul her shirt over her head, tossing it to the ground in a hurry. Her lacy pink bra played peekaboo with what was underneath and hell if he didn't need that off, as well. He reached behind her and unhooked it, letting it fall.

As if needing to reciprocate, her fingers went to the buttons of his shirt and quickly undid them, pushing the fabric off his shoulders. She watched him as he shrugged out of it.

"God, Ellis, you're beautiful," she murmured, her fingers going to his skin and sliding over it. And, damn, it was as sexy as he'd imagined it moments ago.

"Beautiful. Not sure that's the word I'd use."

Her lips touched his chest just above his left nipple. "Oh, but it's the one *I'd* use."

Right now she could call him anything she wanted as long as this moment led to the next and the one after that. He unzipped her slacks and slid them down her thighs. She helped by stepping out of them, leaving her in her very last piece of clothing. And, God, if she wasn't the most gorgeous thing he'd ever seen. Those pink hipster briefs were the same lacy material as her bra had been, cradling her hips and exposing a very sexy bellybutton. He divested

himself of his own trousers, kicking them to
the side before remembering something.

Reaching down, he scooped them back up
and grabbed his wallet, retrieving a packet
from inside as she watched him from beneath
dark lashes. Then before he could say anything, her thumbs hooked in the elastic waist-
line of her underwear, and she pushed them
down in a smooth, sexy move he never could
have imitated. And then they were off and
she was reaching for his briefs.

"Wait. I'll do it." He was less sure of his
control than ever before, and he had no idea
why. He managed to get them off and rip the
condom packet open, sheathing himself.

And then he was back, kissing her, wrapping his arm beneath her buttocks and hauling her against him. And that first touch of
her skin against his was almost more than he
could stand. She was warm and soft, and her
curves cupped him in every way possible.

His mouth went to her nipple, pulling on it
like he'd done with his beer a few moments
earlier, his tongue sliding around the perim-

eter. The gritted sounds she made drove him on as he switched from one breast to the other before the needs of his own body threatened to overwhelm him. He needed this to be soon. He moved back to her lips and kissed her deep and long, his fingers sliding down her belly and finding the juncture between her thighs.

She was warm and wet, and dipping into her was like being wrapped in the finest silk.

"Lyric." He breathed her name as a red haze slowly enveloped him, but still he stayed where he was, stroking her with light touches, letting the sway of her hips guide him as to how soft or hard he went.

She reached for his other hand, twining her fingers in his as her gyrations became more and more sure, quickening her pace as he deepened his. "Oh! Ellis, don't stop. Don't stop..."

No way, sweetheart.

Her hips pushed against him in short jerky movements, seeking what his own body was dying to find. And then it came; he felt it roll over her in a wave that he could no longer resist. He lifted her into position and thrust into her, feeling her spasm against his flesh— molten hot, squeezing him tighter than he'd dreamed possible.

Damn!

He drove into her again and again, the door behind her shuddering in protest. He found her ear, biting the lobe, whispering nonsensical phrases against it that meant nothing and yet everything. A sudden wave of heat rolled through him, scorching everything in its path. His fingers tightened on her ass as he pumped and pumped until he had nothing left to give. And still he continued, desperate not to let this moment end.

But end it did, his breath sawing in his lungs, her arms wrapped solidly around his neck as if holding on for dear life.

He knew exactly how she felt.

Exactly.

And that scared him to death.

Lowering her slowly to the ground with a

groan as he slid free, he tried to wrap his head around what had just happened.

He couldn't.

One moment they'd been looking at a rocking chair and the next...

The rush of pleasure over her reaction to his work. That's what it had been. Except deep down, he knew that wasn't completely true. There'd been that other kiss. The first one. And there'd been no chair in sight that time.

Maybe it was just the combination of everything that had happened over the last little while. That girl's death and Lyric's distress over it. Her surprise over learning that her project was going to be funded by the grant. The trip to the animal shelter and watching her with her niece. All of it had just squeezed up emotion he hadn't known he'd been capable of, balling it all up inside of him until he didn't know his right from his left.

Life was a whole lot easier when he'd had trouble getting attached to things.

Except he'd gotten attached to Max a lot quicker than he'd expected to.

But Lyric wasn't a cat, and getting attached to her or her niece would be...

Impossible.

With his baggage, he wouldn't be good for anyone. Not Lyric. And especially not Alia. So he needed to back off. As fast as he could.

He gathered her clothes without a word and handed them to her, turning his back as he found his own and put them on. When he pivoted to face her, she was pulled back together. Even her hair looked like she'd somehow combed it, the choppy locks all back where they'd been before this...incident.

Incident. That was a good word for it.

He needed to try to explain. To somehow let her know that this couldn't go any further than it had.

"Lyric, listen... I—"

She shook her head. "No, don't. I'm not sure where all of this came from, but it's okay. It happened. We're both adults. We'll just handle this the way adults do."

The same thing he'd told himself a few days ago.

"And how exactly is that?"

"We were both wired from everything that happened. It was going to come out one way or another. Our emotions found the quickest, easiest place and lanced themselves."

Lanced themselves.

Somehow that was not the explanation he'd been going for. "You make it sound like an infection."

She laughed, but it lacked the quick melodic ring of the other one. "Not what I meant— maybe I should have said it was a release valve. Is that better?"

The problem was, it wasn't. But it was as good an explanation as any.

"Yes." He dragged his hand through his hair and looked at her. "So we're good?"

"We are." She paused. "Now that we know this is a problem, we need to be on guard the next time something rises up…" Her voice trailed away—maybe she realized how that sounded.

And actually, he was in danger of something rising up all over again, if he wasn't careful. "Right. We'll be on guard. And make sure this never happens again."

Funny how those words came out sounding less than certain. Probably some crazy part of his brain holding onto the possibility of having sex with her again.

Because that's all it had been. Sex. Just like every other time with every other woman. So there was nothing to be worried about. No unfamiliar emotions boiling out of some secret cavern. Things were just as they always were, except he rarely had sex with coworkers because of how complicated it could become.

But this was different. Because they were on the same page. It was a mistake that wouldn't happen again. He would make sure of it. And he was pretty sure that Lyric would be guarding against any instant replays, as well.

So, yes, they were good.

They'd be able to rebound from this with ease and wind up exactly where they'd started.

* * *

Lyric spent the weekend on edge. What should have been easy to brush off had proven a lot more difficult than she'd thought. Not only had she been mulling over what had happened constantly, but she was also thinking about avoiding him at work on Monday. Or maybe he would be avoiding her. Whichever the case, she dreaded seeing him, which now looked like it would happen the day of the presentation. Ellis hadn't written back with his thoughts, although maybe he'd just been busy and hadn't had time.

But somehow she didn't think so. And if he decided he didn't want to weigh in, she would just have to go with what she had.

Unless she'd somehow blown her chances of getting any of that grant money by sleeping with him. Would he really do that? Withdraw her funding because of a stupid mistake? No, that would be vindictive, and that wasn't like him. She hadn't used what happened against him, nor would she. She'd been just as much to blame as he was. Maybe more. She'd sure

been in a hurry to strip off her underwear…
and his. In fact, he'd tried to stop her, from
what she remembered.

She gulped. Maybe he hadn't wanted to
continue at all, and she'd forced the issue.

Her mind leapfrogged over the events leading up to that moment, and she gave a shake
of her head. No, he'd wanted it. His every
movement had showed just how much. He'd
even said he wanted her.

She shivered as the memory of those
groaned words came back to her.

So what did she do? Text him and ask him
point-blank if she was still invited to the ceremony? Call him and demand to have a face-
to-face meeting?

No. That was one thing she didn't want.
She'd prefer they leave things exactly where
they'd left them. There was no need to revisit
the subject and go over the same ground.

It was a one-time event. It hadn't meant
anything to either of them. They were two
consenting adults who'd shared an hour of
pleasure.

A kind of unearthly pleasure actually. Sex with Jim or anyone else had never been that urgent. That unchained. She was pretty sure Ellis had a bit of a naughty side that he'd reined in, although she couldn't be sure. All she knew was that she'd been willing to experiment with anything he might want to dish out. And that was not like her at all.

Was that a good thing? Or bad.

Maybe it was neither. Maybe it just meant that she'd trusted him not to hurt her, that she believed he was as interested in her pleasure as he was his own. He'd proven that.

Not that it mattered. It was not happening again.

Not. Happening.

"Auntie Lyrie! Shiloh wants a treat."

Alia appeared around the corner, interrupting her thoughts. And she was glad. This was the exact reason sex with Ellis couldn't happen again. She could not risk this little girl being hurt. She'd already been through far more than a four-year-old should ever have to endure. She was not going to put her in a position where she'd experience another loss.

At least not right now. Maybe in a year or two, Lyric would be willing to explore a relationship, and keep Alia out of it until she was very sure it wouldn't implode like it had with Jim.

Ellis is not Jim.

She knew that, but it didn't change the fact that it was too soon. And Alia was too vulnerable. To look to her own needs without thinking about what was in her niece's best interest would be beyond selfish. So she was just going to sit tight. If Ellis wanted to be stupid about this, then she would simply look for a new job and remove herself from the situation.

She'd leave the ball in his court and see what he did.

What about the rocking chair?

She'd make it clear that he didn't have to give it to Alia. In fact, maybe it would be better if he didn't.

"Okay, sweetie. Let's go to the pantry and

get her a treat. And maybe we'll get one for ourselves while we're at it."

Her phone pinged just as she'd sat to watch cartoons with Alia, both of them armed with bowls of vanilla ice cream.

Her heart in her throat, she got up and retrieved the phone from its charger and sat cross-legged on the sofa. Looking down at the screen, she saw Ellis's name in bold print, with the first few words of his text visible.

Just read your...

She clicked on the button to read the rest.

Just read your presentation. All sounds good. Will see you at the ceremony. The address is Fresher Food Products, Inc. Circle 3, Fresher Boulevard. The ceremony will be on the third floor, Room 3B. Any questions, give me a yell. Oh, and bring Alia. No problems there.

She sagged against the couch. So much for not caring whether or not she got the grant money. Of course she did. But even more than that, she'd cared that their time together might have ruptured their working relationship beyond repair. Evidently it hadn't. At least his text seemed to indicate that all was well on that front.

She genuinely liked the man. Respected him. She smiled. That was far removed from her first impression of him. But it was true. And she found that it mattered what he thought of her.

But why? She didn't really care about what Dave Butler thought about her. Maybe because it wouldn't affect her in any real way. She could simply get a new Realtor. But it was a little harder when you were forced to see someone on a daily basis whether you liked them or not.

Or was it more than that?

Ugh, Ly, stop doing this. You're going to drive yourself crazy.

At that moment, Shiloh decided to take a flying leap onto Lyric's arm, knocking her phone away, before she tried to dip her paw into Lyric's bowl of ice cream. "Oh, no, you little varmint. This is mine. You've already had plenty of treats. More than plenty."

Alia was spoiling the cat, but it didn't seem to be affecting Shiloh in any negative way. She was just as sweet and affectionate as she'd been at the shelter. More so, actually. And she was finding the same with Alia. Her niece was becoming more and more loving, adapting to her preschool and home life alike. And where she'd once been fearful and afraid of things that were not familiar, she was starting to explore the world around her with a curious air that made Lyric want to grab the child and hug her tight.

Which is exactly why she didn't want to upset the apple cart. And she wouldn't. Things were back to normal—as in before-sex-with-Ellis normal—and she fully intended to keep them that way.

Monday night came before she knew it, and Lyric smoothed her palms down over her black skirt and the same cream blouse she'd worn to Ellis's house. It was one of her best shirts and worked well in a variety of settings. She wasn't wearing it for him. If anything, she'd torn apart her closet hoping to find something she liked better. But she kept coming back to this same cream top.

And now it was too late to change her mind. Grasping Alia's hand in one of hers while holding the binder with her presentation in the other, she was suddenly a bundle of nervous energy. Why was she even here?

Because a girl had died, drumming into her psyche the need for this program. And chickening out would be both selfish and cowardly.

So she moved to the front desk and signed the register. The attendant issued her a badge. "Do you know where you're going?"

"3B on the third floor, right?"

"That's the one. You have about ten minutes before they start."

She'd cut it close, but was afraid that if she got here a half hour early and had to face Ellis she might actually have some kind of meltdown. She and Alia found the elevator and made their way to the third floor.

As soon as they entered the room, her gaze met familiar green eyes and all the dread she'd pushed down burst back to the surface, where it pooled in her belly and threatened to make her go back the way she'd come. But she didn't. Instead, she moved toward him, forcing a smile that she in no way felt.

"Hi." Her fingers tightened around Alia's hand.

"I wondered if you were going to come."

Perfect. In trying to protect herself she'd put him in the not-so-nice position of having to worry about whether she would put the grant in jeopardy. Not what she'd been going for.

"I'm sorry. I would have texted you if something came up."

"When you didn't respond to my text yesterday, I couldn't help but—" His eyes tracked over her blouse for a second before coming back up to meet her gaze.

She swallowed. He remembered.

Oh, yeah. The shirt had been a mistake. A big one.

Her frozen brain tried to retrace its steps. He'd said something about her not responding. Oh, God, that's right—she hadn't. "I'm sorry. Shiloh actually knocked the phone out of my hand as I was reading your text, and I got distracted. I totally forgot. Thanks for looking the presentation over. I really appreciate it. And I'm really, really nervous, can you tell?"

"I think you're going to rock their world."

His choice of words made her falter even more. Because he'd rocked hers, as well. From the moment he'd walked into it.

He got down on his haunches and met Alia's eyes. "How is Shiloh?"

Tiny fingers squeezed hers even tighter. "Shi Shi loves me."

"Yes she certainly does." He smiled. "Max is doing well, too."

"I like Max." The fingers eased their grip. Lyric hadn't even been sure if the child would remember the other cat once they left the shelter, but she'd asked about him several times. Only there was no way she was going to take her niece to his house to visit. Because it would just bring back memories of what she'd done there.

Because she knew she was in danger of wanting to do it again. That had just been proven when his glance had swept across her shirt and she'd seen the memories parade through those green eyes. Was that why she'd worn it? Because deep down she'd wanted to see if he'd react to it?

Surely not.

God. But what if that really was the reason?

The moderator went to the podium and asked everyone to take their seats. There weren't many people here, maybe fifteen. Lyric wasn't sure if they were all employees of Fresher Foods or if there were other grant recipients besides New Mercy.

She soon had her answer when the speaker mentioned two other organizations that had been awarded matching grants. This food company must have pretty big pockets. Thankfully there weren't a hundred people here. The more intimate setting made it a little less intimidating. At least it would be until they called her name.

Ellis glanced at her and said in a low voice, "Are you okay?"

Not really, but what could she say? *I think I'm falling for you and the ramifications of that scares me to death?*

No. She was not going to confess anything.

"I'm fine. Just a little nervous." She glanced at Alia, who was happily using a blue crayon in her animal coloring book. "Are you sure you don't mind watching her when I'm up there?"

"I don't."

New Mercy would be the last to give their presentations and as she listened to the other recipients she was amazed at the great causes that were out there. Each presenter was eloquent and seemed completely at home speaking before this group; they probably did this all the time. Ellis had said he'd done this before, too.

But she hadn't.

Then it was his turn, and the moment Ellis started talking, she was captivated. This man seemed to master everything he took on with ease. He was a great doctor, was able to turn slabs of wood into gorgeous creations, cared enough for a sick and injured cat to give him a home and had made love to her with a passion that had taken her breath away.

He had. Literally. Taken her breath away.

And right now she having trouble breathing again, because she was very, very afraid that she'd done something irreversible. Something that might destroy everything she'd hoped to build here in Atlanta.

She swallowed. And swallowed again. But she couldn't rid herself of that nagging lump in her throat. The one that bobbed up and down and refused to go away.

She was in love with him.

She couldn't be. She shouldn't be. They'd only known each other a matter of weeks.

But she was. And somehow she was going to have to stop it. Before it got out of control. Before he found out the truth.

All too soon, Ellis was leaving the podium and they were calling her to speak.

Bile rolled around inside of her and threatened to make her bolt from the room. But she couldn't. Alia was here. Even worse, if she ran, he would surely come after her and demand to know what was wrong. And there was no way she wanted him to find out like that. She didn't want him to find out at all.

But he was bound to, wasn't he?

Maybe. But not right now.

She got up and waited until he took her spot next to Alia, who grinned up at him with a smile that nearly broke Lyric's heart. What had she done?

It wasn't about what she'd done. It was now about what she was *going* to do. She couldn't go back to Vegas. So she was going to have to stay here and somehow weather this. Her only saving grace was the fact that Ellis clearly didn't feel the same way about her as she did about him.

She trudged up the steps, knuckles white on her binder as she reached the podium. It was okay. It was going to be okay. She just needed to keep it together.

She opened the binder and started to speak.

CHAPTER ELEVEN

LYRIC HAD DONE an amazing job on her presentation. He couldn't remember ever feeling more proud of someone as she smiled at the right spots and leaned forward to tell Alisha's story to the board members of Fresher Foods. There was a round of applause when she finished, and several people got to their feet.

She walked calmly down the steps and made her way back to where he sat, but there was a stiffness to her that hadn't been there earlier. This was her first time doing this kind of thing, but he was pretty sure it wouldn't be her last, once Jack had heard how well she'd done.

Ellis moved over to take his original seat so she could sit next to Alia. The little girl put her hand in Lyric's and smiled up at her aunt.

He remembered when he'd thought Alia

was like he'd been at her age, losing her mom to circumstances she had no control over. But she wasn't. This child was a lot more well-adjusted than he'd been at her age. He didn't remember much before his mom left, but maybe something had happened even before she'd been taken away that had caused him to be the way he was. Maddie had been a wonderful guardian and in the end her love had helped pull him back from the brink. Maybe it was what had caused him to be a useful member of society. Who knew what he would have become without her.

"You did great, Lyric. Jack and everyone else will be thrilled about the way things went."

She nodded, not quite meeting his eyes. Was she still worried about what had happened between them? She needn't be. After some soul-searching he'd come to the conclusion that it hadn't been the tragedy he'd initially thought. In fact, a tiny portion of his brain had thrown out the idea that maybe it wasn't bad at all. He'd done a lot of changing since they'd first met. Enough to have a shot at a normal life?

Who knew?

Maybe, if they took things slowly, they could see each other socially from time to time and get to know each other.

He would talk to her about it once they got out of here. Except she had Alia with her. So maybe it would be better to wait until tomorrow at work.

Except that wasn't the kind of conversation he wanted to have at the hospital, either. He could ask if he could go back with them to her place to talk. She could put Alia to bed, and he could tell her what he was thinking. But first they had to get through the rest of the ceremony.

And it wasn't quite as short as he'd hoped it would be. There were pictures to be taken. Hands to be shaken. And the board had seemed thrilled that Alia was there, several of them going out of their way to talk to her.

Another half hour went by before it was over. Then they were out of the building and on the sidewalk out front. Lyric started to say goodbye, but he smiled at her and nodded down at Alia. "I actually have something I'd like to talk to you about."

"About the presentation?"

"No. It's actually about…the other night."

She stiffened, her hand going to Alia's shoulder and pulling her close. Maybe she was afraid he was going to say something in front of the child.

"I don't understand."

Somehow he had to undo all of the stuff he'd said the other night, but he wasn't quite sure how to go about it. "I just wanted to clarify a few things, but I'd rather not do that at work if it's okay."

"Definitely okay." She seemed to relax just a bit. "Do you want to come to the house? To talk?"

Hell, hopefully she didn't think he wanted to pounce on her. He did—especially after seeing her in that silky blouse again—but that wasn't his reason for wanting to talk to her. And if he had any hope of testing the waters, he had to do it right this time. Friendship first. And then slowly move forward.

He followed her to her house and spent a half hour visiting with Alia and playing with Shiloh while the child thought of different scenarios and laughed as he acted them out. It was really the first time he'd interacted with a child outside of his office and it was a lot easier than he'd expected it to be. Lyric sat on the couch and watched without saying much, glancing at her watch periodically. Was she grading him?

Finally she got up and announced, "Time for bed, Alia. Say good-night to Ellis and Shiloh."

"But I want Shiloh to sleep with me."

Lyric smiled at her. "We talked about this, remember? If Shiloh wants to sleep with you, she will. We're not going to force her to do something she doesn't want to do."

"Okay..." The word was said with such overt disappointment that he couldn't help but smile. He'd never seen himself as wanting to be a father, but there was a hint of the tide starting to turn in a different direction.

Slowly, Ellis. Or this is not going to work.

He didn't try to insert himself into their bedtime ritual, sensing his presence might not be welcomed. Instead, he went and sat on the couch and waited for Lyric to reemerge.

He liked watching her with Alia. Liked how earnest she was and how much she adored the child, while not giving in to every little whim the little girl had. Like saying she wanted Shiloh to sleep with her.

Lyric had been smart.

If Shiloh wants to sleep with you, she will. We're not going to force her to do something she doesn't want to do.

A good thing for him to remember. This whole half-baked plan of his would only work if Lyric wanted it too. He wasn't going to try to twist her arm or talk her in to something she didn't want to do. If she wanted to explore what had happened between them, she would.

A few minutes later she came back out and glanced at him. "Drink? Sorry I don't have beer, or really anything besides tea, juice or coffee."

"No, I'm good, thanks. Any problems putting her to bed?"

"Not really, she wanted to stay out here with you, but she finally went down." She twirled an earring, and he focused on the act. She was nervous. He smiled. He was a little nervous himself. He needed to do this now, or he never would.

"And you. Do you want to stay out here with me?"

She sat. On one of the chairs, not on the couch next to him. Not a good sign. "I'm not sure what you mean."

He knew she didn't. And he wasn't exactly sure what he wanted. Only that he was willing to explore the possibilities without making any explicit promises.

"I don't think we really resolved what happened the other night. We both talked around it, and maybe even shut things down prematurely."

"Prematurely. How exactly did we do that?"

"Neither one of us expected that night to play out the way it did. I think we were both shocked by how quickly one thing led to another. And the aftermath was…maybe us being afraid to look it in the face and see it for what it was." He pulled in a deep breath. "So what I'd like to propose is that we maybe could go out periodically. Get to know one another. Become friends. And see what happens."

There was a long pause before she responded.

"Friends. You mean like friends with benefits?" The look in her eyes sent ice water shooting through his veins.

"Not exactly. We don't have to do anything more than get to know each other. At least at first."

"So where 'exactly' do you see this 'getting to know each other' going?"

There was something buzzing in the background, but he wasn't sure what it was.

"I don't have a set plan or a timetable. Maybe we'll get to know each other and then decide we have nothing in common. Or... maybe we'll decide we do."

She closed her eyes, and when they re-opened, she leaned forward, her fingers gripping together. "And where will Alia be while all of this deciding is going on? All of the maybe-we-will, maybe-we-won't scenarios."

"I don't follow."

"Ellis, that little girl is my world, and she deserves every tiny bit of happiness I can give her. And that can't happen if there is someone lurking in the background who may or may not become a permanent fixture in her life." She bit her lip. "If I said yes, and we started dating—with or without your 'set plan' in mind, and then you decide it doesn't work for you, what happens to her?"

"Nothing."

"Wrong. You saw her tonight. It would only take a hot minute for her to get attached to you. If—and probably when—this thing falls flat on its face, you won't be the one standing there watching someone she cares about walk away. It'll be Alia... She'll be absolutely devastated." Her voice wavered so much she stopped and took a couple of breaths. "And I'm not willing to put her through that."

An arrow shot straight through him, rendering him immobile for several long seconds. Isn't that what had happened with his mom when he was five years old? Hadn't she turned and walked away from him without looking back? And look how that had turned out. It had almost destroyed him.

Lyric was right. He was not going to be the guy who did that to someone else. And at this moment in time, he couldn't promise her that he wouldn't. He wasn't even sure he was capable of true, self-sacrificing love. But Lyric was. He'd seen it in the way she tried to save her sister—had done everything in her power to get help for her. He also saw it in her love for her niece. She was willing to make whatever sacrifices she needed to make sure that little girl got off to a good start in life.

Wasn't that why he went into pediatrics in the first place?

The least he could do was follow the example she'd set and turn and walk away before it hurt that little girl. Or her aunt.

So he took a deep breath and said the words he needed to say.

"You're right, Lyric. Absolutely right. I'm sorry I didn't see it before now. As far as I'm concerned, this discussion and what we shared the other day never happened. We'll go back to work and put this behind us once and for all. And from this point forward, I think it best if we don't interact outside of the hospital. Dr. Radner can go on the rest of the research trips with you." Each word sent a burst of acid into his stomach, but it was better to do this now than risk hurt to her or Alia further down the line. "She'll be a better judge of the population segment, anyway."

"Thank you for understanding."

He understood. All too well. He only wished he'd seen it before coming over here. Because despite saying that they could go back to working together, he wasn't at all sure that was possible. And so he was going to take some time to think things through before making any kind of impulsive decisions. And he knew the perfect solution for all involved.

The next two days flew by without any sign of Ellis, for which she was profoundly glad. She'd been wracked by uncertainty over the way they'd left things. But what else could she do? To make matters worse, Jack has asked Lyric to stop by his office sometime before five o'clock. Was it about Ellis? Had he somehow found out?

The hours crawled by, and a couple of times she'd been tempted to text Ellis to see if he'd told the administrator about what had happened between them. Maybe he'd seen it as some kind of ethical dilemma.

Although she'd started a text a couple of times, she ultimately didn't want to have to interact with him unless it was absolutely necessary. It hurt too much. He'd as much as admitted that he didn't know how he felt about her. It had been a slap in the face. A reminder of how she'd misjudged Jim, thinking he would eventually want more from their relationship. But it had never happened.

This was best for all involved. Even if it felt like a hot poker being stabbed into her heart.

Finally, around four thirty, she made her way to Jack's office and sat in one of the chairs that were so similar to the ones in Ellis's office.

"I just wanted to congratulate you in person."

She blinked, not sure what he was talking about. "Is this about...?"

"About your presentation? Yes. Ellis said you did an excellent job, that everyone at Fresher Foods loved you."

"Well, I don't know about that..." He'd praised her to Jack? After their talk she was surprised that he had anything good to say about her at all. Then again, maybe he was better at separating his private life from his professional life. A skill she obviously had not developed.

"I called them. And they confirmed everything he said. I just wanted to say how glad we are that you've joined this hospital."

"Well, thank you. I like it here, as well." She hesitated before deciding to say something. "Ellis is a great department head."

"Yes, he has been. His are going to be some hard shoes to fill."

Shock left her speechless for several seconds before she managed to respond. "I don't understand. Is he leaving?"

Jack frowned. "Didn't he tell you? Ellis decided to take a teaching sabbatical. He said something personal had come up, and he needed to take a break from the hospital."

A landslide happened somewhere inside of her, rocks tumbling one over the other and piling up in her stomach until she could barely breathe. Something personal? There was no way that could be a coincidence. He'd left because of the talk they'd had, although he never even hinted that he was thinking about leaving.

"When will he be back?"

"Officially, his sabbatical is for three months, but…"

From the way the administrator's voice trailed away, he didn't think Ellis was coming back. It was there in the fingers tapping on his desk, in the tight set to his jaw.

"Did he say why?"

"Nope. Just that he needed some personal time."

So nothing about her. She should be relieved, but strangely the only thing she felt was regret. "I'm sure he has his reasons."

"I'm sure he does. I just wish he would have told me what they were."

Lyric wasn't about to admit that she was pretty sure she knew the reasons. But to leave the hospital? If anything, he should have asked her to leave instead. But she'd naively believed him when he said they could go back to the way things were.

Or had she? Wasn't that why she'd tried to avoid him for the past couple of days? Which now seemed ludicrous, since he wasn't even at the hospital.

"Where's he teaching?"

"At one of our satellite hospitals in Brunswick."

Wasn't that a long way from Atlanta? She wasn't all that familiar with the geography of the state, but was pretty certain he wouldn't have just moved across town.

No, this was permanent. And she had herself to blame. All she could do was nod her understanding at Jack and excuse herself before she blurted out the truth. Which would help no one. As she left, she tried to tell herself this was for the best, when what she really knew was that she was going to miss him. Terribly.

CHAPTER TWELVE

HER MOM AND dad carried in Alia's birthday cake as they all sang to the child. Her mom had pulled her aside when they'd arrived yesterday and asked if anything was wrong.

Everything was wrong, but crying about it to her mom was not going to change anything. Ellis was gone. Probably for good. And true to what she'd thought, Alia had gotten over him, quickly.

Too bad Lyric hadn't been able to bounce back just as easily. She plastered on a smile and sang the final phrase of the song, clapping along with her parents as Alia blew out the candles on her cake, Shiloh keeping a close eye on the proceedings.

They cut the cake and sat at the table to eat, Lyric telling her parents about everything under the sun except for a certain pediatrician. It would be okay. Eventually. And by the time Ellis came back—*if* he decided to come back—she would be used to living life without seeing him on a daily basis. Surely that would be her new normal, and they would become just two colleagues who'd once done something so incredibly impulsive that they'd be able to laugh about it.

But right now, the last thing she felt like was laughing.

The doorbell rang, snapping her out of her stupor.

"I'll get it," her mother said, heading to the door. She opened it and stood there for a minute or two. "Honey do you have a tip?" The comment was directed at her father.

"I have some money, Mom." She wasn't exactly sure what she needed it for, since they hadn't ordered takeout, and she couldn't remember ordering anything off the internet.

Her dad beat her to the punch, as he always did. But when he came back, he wasn't empty-handed. He was carrying a chair. A familiar, beautiful chair with a wide back and a rocker at the bottom. Across the arms was a big red ribbon and a tag that said, Happy Birthday, Alia.

She stood stock-still. God. She knew that chair. Had sat in it, had slid her fingers over it in his workshop.

It was Ellis's.

Surely he knew she wouldn't expect him to give Alia that chair after all that had happened.

A huge lump formed in her throat as she took off the simple tag and studied the strong slashes that formed the letters. Ellis had written this. He'd had to have gone home to make out the card, at least. But he hadn't delivered it in person.

He'd taken her words at face value. And she'd meant them when she said them, but…

Had she judged him unfairly because of what had happened with Jim, assuming motives where there were none?

But there was still Alia to consider. He could still hurt her without trying.

Hell, so could Lyric. She could do something stupid and hurt her, too. Or her mom or dad or any other human being on the planet. She'd sat there while he talked, but had she really listened, or had she heard only what she wanted to hear? What the filter of the past allowed her to hear?

"This is gorgeous, Lyric. But there's no name on the tag."

Her dad carried the chair to the center of the room. "It looks handmade."

"I know who it's from, Mom. And, yes, it's handmade." She bit her lip, trying to form her thoughts into something cohesive and failing completely. "It was actually made by a friend."

Her mom's face cleared. "A *guy* friend?"

She laughed, although it was shaky. "Yes. A *guy* friend." She turned to Alia. "This is from Ellis. It's for you. He thought you could rock Shiloh on it."

"Ellis has Max."

"Yes, he does." Had he taken the cat with

him to Brunswick? Or was Max at the house by himself?

It was Saturday. Was he home for the weekend?

Suddenly she knew she had to find out. And she wanted to sit down and talk to him and let him explain what he'd meant before. This time, she would listen, not only with her mind, but also with her heart.

"I hate to ask this, but could you both watch Alia for me for about an hour? There's something I need to do."

"Right now?" her dad asked.

Her mom put her hand on his arm with a look. "It's okay, honey. Go."

So she threw a smile at both of them and gave Alia a hug before walking out the door and heading to her car.

Ellis's lathe spun with a fury born out of frustration. And regret. He probably shouldn't have sent that rocking chair to Lyric. She'd made it pretty damn clear that she didn't want a relationship with him, but that didn't mean *he* didn't want one.

Over the past month, his heart had paced in his chest, listing all the reasons they should be together. But none of that mattered, because in the end, she hadn't wanted to be with him. He understood the reasons, but after doing some soul-searching, he realized he would not have just turned and walked out on that little girl. In his heart of hearts he'd believed they should be together. He just hadn't wanted to rush in like a bull in a china shop. And the second he'd said the word *friend* her whole face had changed.

A week after he'd arrived in Brunswick the truth had hit him. He loved her. He'd wanted to take it slow to give himself a chance to adjust to that fact. To believe it was possible for him to love.

Now he knew he could, but it was too late. He carved the spindle to his newest creation, only this time it wouldn't be a rocking chair. He was done with those forever. This time he was making a headboard.

The door to his workshop cracked open a hair and at first he thought Max had somehow gotten out of the house and was trying to get in, until it opened the rest of the way and Lyric stood in the opening.

He stared for a minute before realizing his tool was still spinning, putting a huge gouge in what he'd been working on.

He shut down the machine, the space going quiet in a matter of seconds.

"Did the chair arrive okay?"

"It did. And Alia loves it, thank you." She hesitated then moved farther into the space. "I was hoping you might be home."

"Why?" He didn't move from where he sat. He wasn't sure why she was here, but there was no way he was laying his heart on the table again.

"Because I didn't like the way we left things."

Something began spinning, but it wasn't his lathe this time. It was inside of him. "What part didn't you like?"

She came another step closer until she stood in front of his chair. "The part where you left."

"It's what you said I'd do. I figured better now than later."

"I know I said it. But I think I may have been wrong. My heart didn't want you to go, even though my head said it was for the best." She gave a tired laugh. "I found out that my head doesn't always know what it's talking about."

He sat there for a minute. "Before this goes any further, I need you to know something."

"Okay."

"I do know what it's like to have someone walk away and be the one left standing there. The one who's left devastated."

"You do?"

He shrugged. "My mom left when I was five. She gave me to a friend of hers, and I never saw her again. So, yes, I know what it's like. And when you talked about Alia being hurt, I told myself I wasn't going to be like my mom and cause someone else the pain I'd felt. It was only after I went on sabbatical that I realized I was right. I wouldn't. I would never put someone through what I'd gone through. Especially not a child."

"I think I know that now. I'm sorry, Ellis."

"Don't be. I realize I went about it the wrong way, but I needed to be sure. I had what they called an attachment disorder when I was a child—probably because of what happened—and so it's hard for me to believe in my ability to love. And I didn't want to commit until I knew for sure that I could. That I wouldn't hurt you or Alia."

"I had no idea you'd gone through that." She picked up one of his hands, her fingertips skating across his calluses. "But what if your heart didn't lose its ability to love? What if it just grew calluses to protect itself from being hurt? Like your hands did."

Calluses. He'd never thought about it that way.

She went on. "I think maybe I have calluses, too." She looked him in the eye. "But I no longer want them to stop me from loving. I need to know what you feel for me exactly. And what you hope to feel in the future."

"Why?"

"Because I love you, and I think I shut you out before you could sand those calluses away and discover was underneath them. I meant what I said about Alia. I don't want her hurt, but if you think you could come to love me..."

"I can't 'come to.'" At the stricken look on her face, he hurried to finish. "I can't, because I'm already there. I didn't know for sure the night we talked, but I do now. I'm sorry I wasn't able to express myself well enough to make you understand that I wasn't walking away. I was finally walking *to* something, even if my steps were a little tentative."

"You love me?"

"I do."

Her hand gripped his tighter. "So you're willing to give me—to give us, me *and* Alia—another chance?"

"Only if you're willing to forgive my rough start and trust me to finish well. Trust me to never walk away."

"I do."

He curled his arm around her waist and

slowly reeled her in, before stopping. "Where's Alia?"

"She's at the house. My mom and dad are watching her."

"Your mom and dad. I've met your mom. I guess I should meet your dad, too."

She smiled. "Yes. But not right this second. Right now, I want you all to myself. I love you, Ellis."

"I second everything you just said." He lifted her palm and pressed his lips to it. "From now on we only grow calluses here."

"It's a deal."

This time when he kissed her it wasn't on her palm. It was on her mouth. And when they finally came up for air, Ellis gave her a smile that he hoped contained everything his heart wanted to say. Because he was ready to shed his calluses one at a time and trust that she would wait as he completed the process. Because he had no intention of going anywhere.

He was home. Finally and truly...home.

EPILOGUE

LYRIC PRESSED A protective hand to the rounded bump of her stomach as her husband slowly put his phone on the bedside table. After six months of marriage, they'd decided to add a baby to their little family. She'd also decided to take a leave of absence from her job at the hospital to work on her drug-prevention program, which—while still in its infancy—showed a lot of promise.

"Ellis? What's wrong?"

He lowered himself into the rocker and shook his head. "That was someone from the FBI."

"What?" A spike of fear went through her.

"My mom..."

Ellis had told her the full story about how his mom had been taken away when he was five. She'd been devastated for him, unable to imagine what he must have gone through. At least Lyric knew what had happened to her sister, not that it made it any easier. "Did they find out what happened to her?"

Max came into the room and jumped in Ellis's lap as if he also knew something was wrong. The two cats had both become beloved family members, though it was clear Max loved Ellis the most.

Her husband stroked the cat's fur as Lyric sat across from him on the bed.

His eyes came up and she could swear she saw moisture in those gorgeous green depths. "I think she's alive, Lyric. My mom's alive."

She reached across and gripped one of his hands. "How? Where?"

She wasn't sure whether to be ecstatic or furious with the woman who'd abandoned her own child, leaving him to face a wealth of pain. Alone.

"My father was evidently a mobster. She testified against him. But before she did, she hid me with Maddie and made her FBI handler promise to give me a new identity, along with Maddie and herself."

"And they're just now telling you this?"

"She was convinced my father would try to find me, even from prison, and thought the only way to keep me safe was to leave me behind." He gave a visible swallow. "She sacrificed herself so that I could grow up far away from that life."

Lyric's free hand went to her chest. "That's what I wanted to do for Alia. Get her away from anything that could link her back to my sister and that way of life."

"Exactly."

"Wow, it's so hard to fathom… Where is she?"

"California. My dad died in prison a week ago. So the danger to her is evidently over. She asked her handler to contact me and ask if I wanted to see her."

"You do, don't you?"

"I don't know, Lyric. I really don't."

Her fingers traced the area just below his

fingers with a smile. "Calluses, Ellis. Calluses."

One side of his mouth quirked in that crooked smile she loved so much.

"Point taken. I'm not sure I want her in our lives, though. We're just getting started. And she—"

"She loves you, Ellis. Can you imagine how hard it must have been to leave behind your child, possibly for the rest of your life? To protect him the only way you knew how?"

"I think somewhere along the way, I realized that. On some level. It was the only way I could allow myself the freedom to love you like I do. And I do love you. And Alia and now Sarah."

"I know you do." They'd decided to name the baby after Lyric's maternal grandmother.

"So, you think we should meet her?"

"I do. But if you need some time to process it, it's okay."

He reached up and slid his hand behind her nape, pressing his forehead to hers, even as

Max abandoned his post and stalked from the room. "What did I ever do to deserve you?"

"The same thing I did to deserve you. We're two people in love. And it looks like we may be growing our family in more ways than just this baby."

He pulled back to look at her. "Will you go with me? To meet her, I mean."

"I will if you want me to." She put her finger to his lips. "But as far as names go, you will always be Ellis Rohal to me, no matter what your birth name may have been."

"What if it's something really cool, like Brad or Johnny?"

"I think Ellis is pretty darned cool. And it suits you."

He kissed her. "God, I love you."

"I love you, too."

With that he stood and reached a hand out to help her up. Then they turned and headed out to the living room, where Lyric's mom and dad were playing with Alia and trying to keep Shiloh from chasing Max. Their household was pure chaos, but that was okay, because it was *their* chaos.

And no matter how things turned out with Ellis's mom, they would face it together.

Because that was what love did.

* * * * *

NEATH PORT TALBOT LIBRARY								
AND INFORMATION SERVICES								
1		25		49		73		
2		26		50		74		
3		27		51		75		
4		28		52	6|22	76		
5		29		53		77		
6		30		54		78		
7		31		55		79		
8		32		56		80		
9	2|23	33		57		81		
10		34		58		82		
11		35		59		83		
12		36		60		84		
13		37		61	9|22	85		
14		38		62		86		
15		39		63		87		
16		40		64		88		
17		41		65		89		
18		42		66		90		
19		43		67		91		
20		44		68		92		
21		45		69		COMMUNITY SERVICES		
22		46		70				
23		47		71		NPT/111		
24		48		72				